## Praise for The David Bra

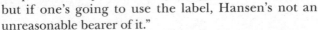

"Read in the order written, [the Brandstetter mysteries] are remarkably linked through symbol, incident, and character, to the point that one sees them as a single, multi-volume novel, by which one may learn a great deal about what it means to be homosexual and male in modern America."

—*The New Republic*

"Hansen is quite simply the most exciting and effective writer of the classic California private-eye novel working today."

—*Los Angeles Times*

"No one in the history of the detective novel has had the daring to do what Joseph Hansen has done: make his private eye a homosexual ... who is both a first-rate investigator and one of the most interesting series characters in the history of the genre."

—**David Geherin,**
*The American Private Eye*

"The first thing I ever read by Joseph Hansen was *Fadeout* (1970). It's the seminal novel in a mystery series about a smart, tough, uncompromising insurance investigator by the name of David Brandstetter. He is a Korean War vet and ruggedly masculine. He's educated, principled, compassionate—but willing and able to use violence when nothing else works. He represents the (then) new breed of PI—the post-World War II private investigator. There are no bottles of rye in Dave's desk, there are no sleazy secrets in his past, and the dames don't much tend to throw themselves at him. He is neither tarnished nor afraid. Oh, and one other thing. He's gay. ... He was not the first gay detective to hit mainstream crime fiction, but he was the first normal gay detective, and that—as the poet said —has made all the difference."

—**Josh Lanyon,**
**from** *The Golden Age of Gay Fiction*

# THE LITTLE DOG LAUGHED

## THE DAVE BRANDSTETTER NOVELS

*Fadeout* (1970)
*Death Claims* (1973)
*Troublemaker* (1975)
*The Man Everybody Was Afraid Of* (1978)
*Skinflick* (1979)
*Gravedigger* (1982)
*Nightwork* (1984)
*The Little Dog Laughed* (1986)
*Early Graves* (1987)
*Obedience* (1988)
*The Boy Who Was Buried This Morning* (1990)
*A Country of Old Men* (1991)

# THE LITTLE
# DOG LAUGHED

# JOSEPH HANSEN

A DAVE BRANDSTETTER NOVEL

SYNDICATE BOOKS
NEW YORK

First published in 1986
by Henry Holt

This edition published in 2023
by Syndicate Books
www.syndicatebooks.com

Distributed by
Soho Press, Inc.
227 W 17th Street
New York, NY 10011

ISBN 978-1-68199-060-6
eISBN 978-1-68199-061-3

Printed in the United States of America

10 9 8 7 6 5 4 3 2 1

*In memory of Eric Walter White*

THE CONDOMINIUMS, RAW cedar beams supporting shake roofs and plank decks, the sun glaring off glass walls, looked easy to get to from the coast road, but there turned out to be gates. Beside these was a raw cedar and glass guardhouse. When Dave drove up and halted the brown Jaguar behind a new BMW, a guard, a tall, lean, white-haired black in wonderfully unwrinkled suntans, stood in the doorway of the guardhouse listening to a stocky woman in suede boots, designer jeans, and a gaucho hat, who was going to lose patience before he did. She was blinking hard. And not just because the wind off the ocean was blowing in her face.

"I tell you, she left specific instructions I was to feed her damned cat." She jerked back the cuff of a fringed leather jacket and read a wristwatch. "At precisely four in the afternoon, every damned day. And water the plants."

"She didn't leave those instructions with us." The guard tried a smile of regret and sympathy. "I'm sorry. Her husband—Mr. Gernsbach—he didn't say nothing, either."

"But the damned cat will starve," the woman cried. She dug into a shoulder bag, came up with keys, jingled them in the man's face. "She gave me her door key. What more proof do you want?"

"Don't you worry," the guard said. "We'll feed the cat."

"She has to be petted, too," the woman said.

"That cat?" The man gave a little dry laugh. "No, ma'am. Not that cat. You try petting her, she turn around and rake your hand open."

"Oh, you know her, do you?" The woman dropped the keys back into the bag. "I don't know why Lily keeps her. Pedigree is one thing, but she's not civilized."

"Pretty, though," the guard said. "We'll feed her."

"And water the plants?" the woman said.

"Yes, ma'am. Thank you for calling it to our attention."

The woman seemed uncertain. She started to speak again, then saw Dave waiting. Turned, turned back, and at last got into the BMW, slammed the door in annoyance, and drove off.

"Yes, sir?" the guard said. "Who did you wish to see?"

"I have an appointment with Christina Streeter." Dave laid a business card in the guard's hand. He read it, stepped up into the guardhouse, took down a telephone receiver there. He pushed buttons, waited a long time, spoke into the receiver, and hung it up again. "She's expecting you," he said.

"What kind of cat is it?" Dave said.

"Big orange-color Persian," the guard said. "One of those with a little pug nose and big saucer eyes. Beautiful. Her mama and papa were both champions, blue ribbons galore. She worth a lot of money." He laughed and wagged his head. "But she sure grumpy." He reached for something inside the guardhouse. "Grumpiest cat I ever did see."

Dave got into the Jaguar, slammed the door. What the guard had reached for was a switch. An electric motor whined, and the high wire-mesh gates that matched the razor-wire-topped fencing that surrounded the place swung open. He took a curving drive of cleanly swept fresh blacktop and parked in a square surrounded by azalea bushes. The shadows of gulls flickered over him as he walked among carefully tended plantings to the door marked twenty-seven in brass numerals. He pushed a button under a hanging wooden cricket lantern whose paper panels wind and seaspray had shredded. An electronic chime pinged inside. And in half a minute, the door was opened by a scrawny six-foot adolescent in wet, floppy swim trunks, a blend of purples, magentas, and pinks, all faded. He was drying spiky red hair with a yellow-and-green-striped towel. Acne flared angrily on his face, neck, shoulders. He squinted at Dave against the sun.

"Brandstetter," Dave said. "To see Miss Streeter?"

"Oh, hi," the boy said indifferently, and turned away to call, "Chrissie? It's the insurance guy." He stumped away on skinny bow-legs, telling Dave, without looking back at him, "Come on in." He disappeared up a spiral steel staircase.

Dave came in and shut the door. The room was down a couple of steps from the entryway. The furniture was Chinese, carved wood, lacquered black. The rug was Chinese, too, old, camel's hair, quiet designs in blue and rose, the biggest Chinese rug Dave had ever seen, and beautifully kept. The splayed wet footprints of the acned boy lay on it like blasphemy. The room was a great square, shadowy under beams and lofts and skylights two stories overhead. A large bronze Buddha sat with crossed legs, hands together, palms up in his lap, and smiling serenely. Not Chinese. Burmese, perhaps. Superb gold lacquer cabinets of silk stretched on bamboo rested their fragility on low ebony stands. A Japanese screen pictured a procession among mountains. Over the fireplace hung a Tibetan banner of some fierce, fanged demon, once borne aloft in parades.

At the far end of the room, French doors opened on a patio where a swimming pool shone an unreal blue back at the unreal blue of the sky. A slim, dark girl in a white bikini appeared in the doorway and stood there, flapping into a white terry cloth robe and stretching her neck a little, seeming to peer into shadows darker than those the room created. She then drew dark glasses from a pocket of the robe, put them on, and, from where it leaned in the doorway without Dave's having noticed it, groped out for and found a slender white cane with a red tip. She stepped down into the room, barefoot as the boy had been, and came toward Dave, smiling, moving the cane at about shin level back and forth in front of her, and tracking damp footprints on the priceless rug as the boy had done.

"Mr. Brandstetter?" She stopped a yard off, and he saw that he had been mistaken about her smile. It was not a smile. It was some sort of habitual grimace that had to do with her not being able to see, a kind of wince, maybe, already in place for the moment when she ran into something. In fact, when she stopped moving, and the grimace went away, her expression was sad. "You said you had questions. I thought I'd answered every question there could be. For the police."

"I've read their report," Dave said. "I'll try not to ask the same things again."

She sighed and gestured with the slim cane at one of two long couches that faced each other with coffee tables in between, lamps at either end. One couch was cushioned in a nubby wool dyed the same quiet blue as that in the carpet, the other in the same quiet hue of rose. It was the rose-color couch she pointed at. "Will you sit down?"

"Thank you." Dave went past her and sat. She seemed to listen to his passage, as if she could detect a turbulence in the air around him. Certainly the carpet didn't allow his footfalls to sound. When he sat, the cushions received his weight without comment. She seemed to know exactly where he was even before he spoke. She sat at the other end of the couch and turned her sad face with its big dark glasses resignedly toward him. Dave said, "Do you think your father killed himself?"

She gave a little bleak shrug. "They told me the gun was in his hand. There were powder burns on his hand. And at his temple, where the bullet went in." She braced a foot on the handsome coffee table, leaned forward, and dried her toes with a corner of the robe. "I guess he killed himself. But I don't know why."

"He wasn't depressed?" Dave said. "He wasn't in some kind of trouble you know about?"

"He was angry at my mother." Chrissie gave a mirthless little laugh. "But he was always angry at her. She was raising hell. Again. About me. I'm a bone of contention between them." She dried the other set of toes, then drew her legs under her on the couch, pulling the robe across them as neatly as if she could see. "I mean—I was. I don't know what's going to happen to me now. My father had custody, you see. He had Brenda ruled unfit by a court. She drank and popped pills. Still does. Judge Farmer made her check into a hospital, but after she came out, she started right in again, same as before. It's not her fault. It's a sickness."

"You'll be all right," Dave said.

"Not unless I get married, I won't be," she said.

As if this were his cue, the gangly boy came down the stairs, barefoot but in floppy camouflage pants now, and a camouflage tanktop he had scissored short just below his ribs. His shoulders were spare as coat hangers. He had blow-dried his Raggedy Andy hair. A strong deodorant smell came off him. When he got to the foot of the staircase, he mumbled without looking their way, "Anybody want a soda?" and before he got an answer, went off out of sight behind the broad mellow-brick wall that held the fireplace.

"He looks too young to marry," Dave said.

"He is," Chrissie said. "A year younger than me. Sixteen." She twitched Dave a smile. "Are you single, by any chance?"

"That's the nicest offer I've had all day," Dave said. "But we hardly know each other. What about your father's work? Was there something wrong with that?"

"Everything was great. He just got a hundred thousand dollars from cable TV for a series of articles he did a year ago for the *New York Times* Sunday magazine. On Cambodia.

They're going to make a mini-series." She laughed. "He bought French champagne and opened a big can of caviar they gave him in Russia when he was doing that Siberian railway story." She giggled. "First time I ever had champagne. First time I ever had caviar. I don't know if I like caviar. But I like champagne. If I wasn't afraid of getting like Brenda, I'd have champagne for breakfast every day."

"It gets expensive," Dave said, "does French champagne."

It couldn't rightly be said that she looked at him, could it? Or looked away, when she looked away. She turned her face away, and said to the beautiful room, "I can afford it." There wasn't much happiness in the statement. It was just that. Her fingers found the end of the terry cloth sash and fiddled with it. "Gandy died last week," she said.

Dave frowned. "Gandhi died forty years ago."

"Not him. My grandmother. I couldn't say *grandma* when I was little. I said *Gandy,* and it stuck, you know? She left me everything. That's why Brenda wants me back. If she was my legal guardian, she'd have control of the money."

"Maybe she loves you," Dave said. "Mothers have been known to do that."

The boy came back, holding three dewy soda cans in his knuckly hands, and set them on the coffee table in front of the rose-color couch among a scattering of netsuke, little yellow and white and brown ivory carvings of monkeys and mice and insects. He sat on the floor. "Not her mother," he told Dave. "Her mother's a witch."

"What about her father?" Dave said.

"I didn't know what the hell he was talking about half the time," the boy said, "but you had to like him. He didn't act old, you know. He watched me skateboard a little out there in the parking space one day, and said could he try it, and he was as good as I was. Right away, man. No practice. He was flaky. He stood on his head for five minutes every morning—said it prevented kidney stones." The boy reached for one of the soda cans and drank from it. "He did those Chinese exercises, tai chi, where you make gestures"—he stretched out an arm, and soda slopped from the can and splashed on the carpet—"in slow motion, right? Almost like dancing. He said it will keep you alive and healthy till you're a hundred and ten years old."

"Not him," Chrissie said. Slow tears ran down her face.

"Oh, Jesus," the boy said. "I'm sorry. I forgot."

"It's all right," she said. "I like to hear you talk about him. Go on."

"He always used a typewriter," the boy said. "Electric, sure, but really old. I mean, it didn't even have a type ball. It had keys, okay—clackety-clack? Really noisy. And the one he took on trips was even older. The cloth was coming off the case in shreds. He went everywhere, man. All over the world, wherever there was trouble. When they blew up those Marines in Lebanon, he was there. He actually saw that damned truck loaded with explosives when that crazy—"

"He wasn't that close," Chrissie said. "Don't exaggerate. Tell about the word processor."

"I'm a computer freak." The boy gulped more soda. "Have been since I was five. And I made fun of those typewriters. I said he could work faster and turn out more stuff if he had a word processor. And he said, 'Will you teach me how to use it, Dan'l?' That's really my name—Dan'l. And I told him I'd try, only maybe he was too old to learn." Dan'l barked a laugh at himself. "Hell, he caught on in about half an hour. He was sharp."

"For an old guy," Dave said.

Dan'ls acne grew redder. He stared large-eyed at Dave and his larynx bobbed. "Oh, hell. I keep putting my foot in my mouth."

"He was only forty-two," Dave said. "It happens fast. And it happens to everybody. Even you."

"Not forty-three," Chrissie said softly. "Not to Adam."

"What was he working on?" Dave said. "Or was he coasting for a while on that big check from the cable people?"

Chrissie groped out toward the table. Dan'l sat forward on his skinny butt, reached the second soda can for her, and put it carefully into her hand. The fingers of her other hand explored the wet top of the can to find the opening. She drank. "He was working," she told Dave. "He didn't know how to stop. He was as bad about that as Brenda is about drinking. I think one caused the other. But I don't know who started first. Him, probably. She hated for him to go away all the time, and he kept promising her he wouldn't but he kept going anyway."

"Working on what?" Dave said.

"Something about Central America. He was speaking a lot of Spanish lately. On the phone. Central America's where the action is, right now. Like Dan'l said, that's what he always worked on. The trouble spots."

"Nicaragua?" Dave said. "El Salvador?"

Chrissie shook her head and frowned. "Another one. Los Inocentes? That's the one. It's a funny name for a whole country—Los Inocentes. The innocent ones?"

"It was discovered by Balboa in 1513," Dave said, "on a religious holiday—the Feast of the Holy Innocents. He claimed it for Spain. That's what he named it when he planted the flag on the beach. That's why."

"You sure you don't want to get married?"

"I'm too old for you," Dave said. "Your father didn't tell you anything about his Inocentes story?"

"There are rebels." Dan'l sucked soda from the can and wiped his chin. "Communists. They're trying to take over the government. The government sends out death squads and murders people in villages for helping the rebels. And if the villagers don't help the rebels, the rebels kill them. I saw it on TV."

Chrissie coaxed Dave, "I'm going to be very rich."

"That's nice, but I'm all right for money. I inherited stock in a very big insurance company."

"The one you're here for?" She was surprised. "Banner?"

"Not that one," he said. "Medallion. My father built it. Anyway, I wouldn't marry you for your money. What do you think I am?"

"A very nice man," she said, "and very intelligent."

"And old enough to be your grandfather," he said. "I almost never travel. I rarely stand on my head, except figuratively. And if I tried to ride a skateboard I'd break my neck. For whom was he writing this piece on Los Inocentes?"

Chrissie had a mouthful of soda. She shook her head and swallowed quickly. "He hadn't sold it. He didn't want anyone to know about it. Not yet. There was one thing he still had to confirm. When he had that, it would be the hottest story of the decade. That's what he told me." Her voice caught, and tears ran out from under the dark glasses again. "That was the last thing he said to me."

"Don't cry, Chrissie." Dan'l came around the table to her on his knees, and wiped her tears with clumsy fingers. "It won't bring him back."

She pushed his hands away. "It's not that. Brenda's going to get me, Dan'l. He can't stop her now. Gandy can't. Nobody can."

Dave stood up. "I'd like a look at his workroom, if that's all right."

"We can run away," Dan'l said. "His car's still here."

She laughed. It was a doleful sound. She groped out and stroked his hair. "Aw, Dan'l—they'd put me in jail for child stealing." She located her cane and stood up quickly. "Come on, Mr. Brandstetter." Swinging the red tip of the cane from side to side, inches above the carpet, she moved off toward the staircase.

## 2

THE WORKROOM WAS up two flights, at the rear of the house, so its French doors overlooked the patio with the swimming pool. The furnishings here were mostly Middle Eastern—lots of mother-of-pearl inlay and pierced brass. The carpet was Persian, in rich wine reds. He crossed it, among low tables and cabinets, one of which housed a television set, to stand at the doors. Outside, a small balcony was crowded with plants in pots. Two pots had fallen off the flat rail and broken. Plants in pots hung by bristly macramé cords from overhead rafter ends. Across the patio, beyond the panes of French doors like these, a fluffy orange cat lay on a bed and stared out at the fine day with big golden eyes.

"That's the Gernsbach place over there," Dave said. "Nice people," Chrissie said. "They've gone on a trip."

"Not the cat," Dave said.

"She's a terrorist," Dan'l said. "She'd hijack the plane."

This place and the Gernsbach place were the only ones that opened on the patio. The other walls were blank, one of them climbed by a vine with hot red flowers. Dave turned to look at Adam Streeter's workroom—file cabinets, bookshelves, a long desk on which sat a word processor with a blank gray screen. A square white printer squatted beside it. Chrissie leaned back against the desk, absently thumbing the corner of a thick annual reference book that lay there. Bits of paper stuck out of the book, marking pages. Dave asked her, "When did they leave?"

"He was already gone when I found Adam dead." Chrissie sounded numb. "He was the first person I thought of, the nearest, the kindest. But when I got there, Lily said he'd left on a trip, and she was going to join him."

"Mr. Gernsbach," Dave said.

"Harry," she said. "Lily phoned the police for me. I didn't know what to do." She laughed sadly. "I still don't."

"Stop worrying," Dave touched her shoulder. "I know Judge Farmer. I'll speak to him."

"Will you?" she said. "I can look after myself here."

Dave wondered why no papers lay on the desk. The house was beautifully kept. Was Streeter just as compulsively neat about his workplace? Dave opened desk drawers. Passports, plane ticket envelopes, bills, receipts, canceled checks lay in one; pens, paper clips, postage stamps, rubber bands, scissors, staple gun cluttered another. But not a page of manuscript, not a scribbled note. No cassettes, no diskettes. He checked out the file cabinets. Clippings in folders, manuscripts of old stories, copies of papers and magazines that had printed them. But nothing on Los Inocentes. He pushed the file drawer shut. Dan'l leaned loosely in the doorway. Dave said to him, "Journalists use notebooks, and if they don't, they use cassette recorders. I don't see one. I don't see any cassettes."

Surprised, Dan'l came into the room a few steps and peered around puzzledly. "He had a couple recorders. Little ones, good ones," The boy crouched and opened a Turkish cabinet. The lacy hanging pulls of its double doors rattled. Except for a stack of books, it was empty. The books were in identical shiny jackets. Dan'l said, "Geez, I guess the police took the cassettes and stuff. This was so full, junk fell out of it every time he opened it." He held out one of the shiny books. "He wrote this. You want a copy? There's plenty."

"Thank you." Dave accepted the book scarcely noticing. The report he had read at LAPD this morning had made no mention of Streeter's papers, files, cassettes. Dave said, "What about storage disks? Did he keep those in there, too?"

Dan'l nodded. "That's right." He closed the cabinet, remained crouching, staring at it for a moment, then snapped his fingers and stood up smiling. "I know. He packed them. He was going to take them with him." Dan'l jogged out of the workroom and along a gallery to a room at the front. It was a bedroom. And on the bed lay pieces of soft leather luggage, lids open, half-packed. Curtains were closed across the windows. Dan'l found a pushbutton, a small motor sang, and the curtains parted on a wide blue sky over a narrow blue marina where white pleasure-craft waited under blue wraps, with gulls perching on their mast-tops. While Dan'l ran his hands among the folded clothes in the grips, Dave asked Chrissie:

"This room has a better view. Why didn't he work here?"

"It kept reminding him the world was wide," she said. "And he hadn't seen half of it yet. It made him want to buy a boat and sail around the world. He couldn't sit and put words on paper, looking at this view." Her face was turned toward the light, and she smiled a little wistful smile. "The way he described it, I could almost see it."

Dave looked at it for her. Condominiums not unlike these stood on the marina's far side, and more moored boats. Then there rose green hills, soon to be tawny in the dry heat of summer. On the hills, toy-size at this distance, shone the white Spanish-style buildings of a college. Farther away still, jet liners rose silent from the airport and made wide, lazy curves out over the ocean.

Chrissie said, "I heard him come in, about three." She moved to the bed, sat on a corner of it. "He'd said he might not make it back, might sleep in a motel. It was a long drive."

"To where?" Dave said.

She gave her head a mournful shake. "He wouldn't tell me. He said it would be better if I didn't know. For my own safety. We were out by his car. It was then that he said this could be the biggest story of the decade."

"There's no cassette recorder here," Dan'l said. "None of the junk from the cabinet."

"Since he'd come in so late," Chrissie said, "I didn't bring him coffee right away in the morning. I had my own breakfast first. Then I tapped on the door here, and listened. I have good hearing, and I didn't hear him breathing. So I tiptoed in and touched the bed, and all that was on it was luggage. Which I knew wasn't there when he'd driven off."

"Maybe he bought that plane." Dan'l looked at Dave. "He was talking about having his own plane to fly where he wanted himself instead of on airlines. More mobility, easier access to places they don't let reporters into." He gestured at the pathetic grips. "Maybe he was going to fly to Los Inocentes."

"Poor Adam," Chrissie said softly, and raised her face to Dave. "Anyway, I wondered why he wasn't sleeping. And I thought maybe he'd got the part of the story he needed, and he was so excited he couldn't sleep. It happened sometimes—he'd work all night. So I went to the workroom. The door was closed. I never bothered him in there, but I was worried. I didn't hear a sound inside. I knocked and called him, but he didn't answer. So I went in. I missed him with my cane, and I tripped over him. He was lying on the floor. When I touched him, he was cold. It was no use calling him, shaking him." Her voice went thin and small. "He was dead."

"You hadn't heard anyone else in the house?"

"Not even the gun going off."

"That was because of the silencer," Dave said. "He didn't tell you who he was driving so far to see that day? You don't remember any names from the story he was working on, not one?"

"Two. I overheard him talking to Rue Glendenning—a boy just out of UCLA. A journalism major. They come to

Adam sometimes for career advice. And one of the names was Cortez-Ortiz. The other was really strange." Her clear forehead wrinkled, and she nibbled at her lower lip. She took a deep breath and spoke the word slowly—"Tegucigalpa. Is that right?"

Dan'l laughed. "Sounds like what a turkey says."

Dave said, "The curtains are open on the French doors in the workroom now. Would you know if they were open when you found your father's body?"

"I know," she said, "because I went to them to shout for Harry. The curtains were open, so were the doors. But not across the patio. Mostly they're closed. To keep the cat in. Trinket. She's never allowed out. I realized that after a moment. The Gernsbachs couldn't hear me."

"This trip of theirs," Dave said. "Where did Mrs. Gernsbach tell you they were going?"

"She didn't. Only that it was a very sudden decision. He left first, so I guess it was on business."

"What business would that be?" Dave said.

"Savings and loans," she said. "He's operations manager for one of them. Pacific Sphere? Some name like that."

"He's got a great computer setup over there," Dan'l said. "Interfaced with the ones at his offices."

Chrissie went on, "See, Lily'd been over in Altadena with her mother for a few days. And when she got home, here was this note from Harry. She was awfully upset. Lily hates having to rush."

"Maybe it was to Washington," Dave said. "Congress is investigating savings and loan operations these days. I'd like to talk to them."

"Me, too." Chrissie sighed. "I wish they hadn't gone."

"Tegucigalpa is the capital of Honduras," Dave said. "I don't know what Cortez-Ortiz is. Or who."

"No," Chrissie said absently. Then she stood up. "I know who'll have his papers and things. Mike Underhill."

Dan'l made a sour mouth and groaned. "That creep. I wouldn't trust him with anything of mine."

Dave wouldn't either. It took him a moment, but then he attached the name. Underhill was a flashy journalist who, a few years back, had written a biography short on facts and long on fantasy of a reclusive Texas billionaire, had lived high on a big publisher's advance in Ischia and Saint-Tropez, and then had been jailed for a year on fraud. The book was scrapped, and Underhill was made to repay the publisher's half million. Had he done it? Was he still trying? Who would give him a job, a paycheck?

"Adam trusted him," Chrissie said. "He said somebody had to. Mike had had a rotten break, was all. Those kinds of books are always half made up. Who cared? But Mike wasn't Truman Capote or Norman Mailer. He didn't have a big name. And instead of some crazy murderer, he chose the richest man in the world, and, of course, he got the shaft. Adam said it wasn't fair."

"And he had Underhill working for him?" Dave said.

"Not full time. Just once in a while. But he was here the day before Adam took that drive. Adam must have given him the material—his notes and things."

"To work up?" Dave wondered. "While your father flew to Los Inocentes?"

Dan'l said grimly, "You better get them back, Chrissie. If you don't, he'll write the article, claim it was his, and never mention Adam. Take all the glory for himself."

"I'll dress," she said, "and we'll go." She started for the bedroom door, the gallery that looked down on the tranquil Chinese room far below. "The car keys are in the kitchen."

"Great." Dan'l went out after her. "I love to drive that car. It's awesome." He got into step beside her. "You want me to guide you down?"

"I'll do that." Dave followed them. "You go ahead. I have some more questions for Chrissie."

"I can go downstairs by myself," she said.

"I'll get the car." Dan'l swung down the corkscrew stairs like a playground child, bare heels making the treads gong.

16

"What questions?" Chrissie groped out to find the slim black rail with thin fingers. Once she had the rail to steer by, she went down almost as briskly as Dan'l. Dave followed. "I sleep down here, at the front, under Adam's bedroom."

"And above the front door," Dave said, "so it was easy to hear him come in the other night, morning. These stairs are noisy. You heard him climb them?"

"Yes." She took another step down, then stopped and stood motionless. "But nobody else. That's what you want to know, isn't it?" She turned her head, raised it to him. "You don't think he killed himself. You think someone killed him."

"It's a dangerous world," Dave said. "That was what he liked about it—isn't that what you said?"

"He had friends all over that world." She started on down again. The cane hung from her wrist on a loop. Now and then it rang against the ironwork. "They might hate each other—Israelis and PLOs, the IRA and the British, antinukers and generals—but they all liked Adam Streeter." She reached the gallery and started along it toward the front. "He was a journalist, Mr. Brandstetter. He didn't take sides. If he did, how could he work? He didn't have enemies."

A voice came up from below. "He had one, Chrissie."

A sound snagged in Chrissie's throat, and she stopped so abruptly that Dave bumped into her. He looked down. A woman in red stood in the center of the lovely room, gazing up with a mocking smile. Years had marred her looks, but she had been beautiful once and, before that, pretty in the same dark way as Chrissie. There was no mistaking that they were mother and daughter. What time did to some of us!

Dan'l called, "I'm sorry. I tried to keep her out."

"Pack your things, Chrissie." The woman's voice was brittle and bitter and heedless.

She marched for the stairs. "You'll be living with me now."

"I'm all right here, Mother," Chrissie said.

17

"Nonsense—you're helpless." The woman's shoes clanged on the stairs. "I tried to make that senile judge understand that. That your father would be gone half the time. You can't manage on your own."

"I'm helping her," Dan'l said.

The beat of the woman's shoes stopped. "Don't be ridiculous," she said. "You're only a child. And so is she. And children need their parents." She began to climb again. "Especially blind children."

"I'm not a child," Chrissie cried. "I'll be eighteen next year. Go away, Brenda. You have no right to be here."

"No right?" Brenda climbed again. "I'm your mother. Who has more right than that?" She reached the gallery. Temper had got her up the stairs, but she was winded. "Anything could happen to you alone here." She stood panting, hanging on to the flat glossy gallery railing. "Go on." She jerked her chin toward the far bedroom. "Start packing. I'll come in a minute and help you."

"I'm not leaving with you," Chrissie said. "The court took away your rights. If you've forgotten that, I haven't. It was the happiest day of my life."

"Hear that?" The woman said this with a wry smile to Dave. "That's daughterly love these days. Who are you?"

Dave told her. "I'm investigating his death. It's routine."

She scowled. "You mean there won't be any insurance? That's what you mean, isn't it?" She advanced on him. Dave smelled gin. "When they commit suicide, you don't have to pay."

"That's all you think about," Chrissie said. "Money. It's all you're here for. You don't want me living with you. It's Adam's insurance you want, it's Gandy's money."

"Gandy was my mother," Brenda Streeter said. "That money should have come to me, and you know it. I was Adam's wife, you little bitch, for sixteen hellish years. He owed me that insurance money. I earned it." Her laugh was rough with resentment. "Oh, did I ever! What did you ever do for him but depend, depend, depend?"

"He never complained," Chrissie said.

"Ha! Why should he? He could walk out anytime he wanted, and stay away for months. Karachi. Danang. Sidon. I was stuck with you. Every damn day. Twenty-five hours a day."

"You're drunk." Chrissie turned and headed for her room, whose door stood open, bright with sunshine. She guided herself with a hand on the gallery rail. "I'm phoning security. Do you want to leave first, or wait for Mr. De Lis to throw you out?" Dan'l came at a run up the stairs.

Brenda jeered, "Mr. De Lis let me in. He had no choice." She dug in a red shoulder bag, pulled out a paper, flapped it. "I have a court order, signed and sealed. Making me your temporary guardian now that your father is dead."

Chrissie had stopped, turned back. "You can't have. Judge Farmer wouldn't do that to me. He knows what you are."

Brenda's laugh had a jagged edge. "Judge Farmer is dead, Chrissie." She jammed the court order back into the bag, stepped around Dave, strode toward the girl. "I'm surprised you didn't know that, since he was such a friend to you." She gripped Chrissie's arm.

"Leave her alone." Dan'l darted past Dave, caught Brenda from behind, pulled her off balance. With a cry, she sat down hard on the hard, shiny planks of the gallery.

Grunting, she struggled to get to her feet. "You vicious brat. Get out of here." Dave went to help her up. She batted his arm away and snarled, "Keep your hands to yourself. I don't like you." She caught the railing, dragged herself to her feet, stood swaying, pushing messily at her hair. A puddle glistened on the planks where she had sat. A blotch darkened the back of her skirt. "Go away, both of you." She took Chrissie's arm again. "This is between me and my daughter."

Dan'l asked Dave tearfully, "Can't you do anything?"

Dave watched the woman tug the girl away. "Maybe later. Come on. I'll have to drive them. She's too drunk."

They went to wait in the kitchen. Dan'l moodily drank soda. The kitchen was teakwood and copper with accents in Chinese red. Dave smoked. The women's voices came down to them, edgy but faint. Misery was on Dan'l's face, along with the acne. He picked at the sores. Small birds squabbled in the patio shrubs. He watched them. He said to Dave:

"Silencer? You can't put a silencer on a revolver."

"It wasn't a revolver. It was a Desert Eagle. Semi-automatic. Gas-operated, .357 Magnum."

"All he owned," Dan'l said, "was a .32 Colt. I know. He taught me to shoot with it." Dan'l twitched a little smile. "That didn't go over too well with my mom."

"I didn't see his address book up there," Dave said. "Do you know where Mike Underhill lives?"

"In Venice," Dan'l said. "Amoroso Street."

3

It was a narrow street of rundown frame bungalows and big dark acacia trees. Because it was a short walk from the beach, cars lined the curbs, bumper to bumper. This left only a narrow strip to drive. Police department signs warned against parking before nine and after five. Dave read his watch. It was ten past five right now, but only one hairy youth in cracked sunglasses was trying to get off the street, having a bad time with only inches between his dusty Honda CVCC and cars in front and back.

Dave spotted the address Dan'l had given him. In corroded metal numbers on a plywood rectangle hung by wire to a four-foot-high hurricane fence. A shiny lavender van with new paper license plates was parked across the driveway. He wheeled the Jaguar slowly around the block, past a graffiti-scrawled little mom-and-pop grocery, a liquor store with steel-barred windows, the foggy plate glass of a pizza stand, a Laundromat, a bicycle shop, a cave-dark arcade where the lights of electronic games winked and twinkled. This was a long way from Saint-Tropez. How was Underhill liking it?

The van still sat across the driveway, but three cars had taken off from Amoroso Street now, and others were working at it. He slid into a space where the untrimmed and very leafy branches of a big oleander brushed the car. It was risking a ticket, leaving the car here now, but there was no place else to leave it. He was a few doors past the house. The sidewalk was cracked and humped by the roots of the old trees. Under the trees and oleanders, the parking strip was bare of grass and strewn with beer cans and wine bottles in rumpled paper sacks, with crushed Big Mac and Marlboro boxes, bones of Kentucky Fried Chicken, greasy paper napkins. A ragged old man with a filthy white beard came slowly at Dave, pushing a rusty shopping cart crammed with clothes, newspapers, bulgy supermarket sacks. Dave stepped out of his way. He asked for a quarter. Dave gave him a dollar.

The woven wire fence had a gate, but it wouldn't open. It was padlocked. To the woven wire of the gate was fastened a metal sign: No Agents Peddlers Solicitors. Not Beware Dog, but a big white woolly dog jumped at the front window of the house now, and barked. It was a long time since Dave had vaulted a fence. He was going to feel stupid if he didn't manage it. Raw ends of the steel mesh could rip his clothes. He was getting old, and old bones broke easier than young ones. But he gripped the gritty top bar of the fence that held the wire fabric, bent his knees a couple of times, took a deep breath, and swung up and over the fence.

He didn't land gracefully. Still, he was where he wanted to be. He got up a little shakily off the Bermuda grass and brushed at his pants legs with hands that stung where he'd come down on them. He weighed no more today than he had at seventeen. The only time he'd been heavier was in Germany, after the war, a kid lieutenant in Army intelligence, questioning frightened civilians on their political past. None of them had been a Nazi—of course not. And while they scrabbled in the snowy rubble for food, US Army chow was plentiful, and Dave had got up to a hundred-eighty. Duke Summers, his skinny sidekick, had nicknamed him Porky.

Before, and since, Dave had weighed one-sixty. So why had he landed so heavily here? Why had he brushed that low fence? With a shake of his head and a glum laugh at himself, he started for the bungalow. The dog left the window and began raving and clawing behind the front door. Dave set a foot on a sagging wooden step, its green paint crackled, and a voice called to him. He paused and looked.

A young Oriental woman regarded him from the driveway. She was brown-skinned and trimly made, and wore white short-shorts, a man's shirt knotted under neat breasts, a rice-paddy straw hat, and straw sandals. From her hand hung a woven straw carryall. "Is it really Hunsinger you are looking for?" she said. "People who need Hunsinger put their clothes on backward and can't tie their shoes." She smiled.

"I'm looking for Mike Underhill," Dave said.

"Ah." She seemed cheered up. "You have an appointment?"

Dave went away from the short green steps, and the dog left off barking and returned to the front window where it stood up with paws on the sill, whimpering, and watching Dave cross the grass to the young woman. Dave told her, "No, I don't have an appointment. Do I also have the wrong address?"

"Not quite. People just forget sometimes to add the one-half after the number. It's the house in the rear. But it doesn't help if he isn't coming." She looked mournfully back along the broken cement strips of the driveway. "He's gone."

"Where to—do you know?" Dave said.

"I don't know. I wanted to talk to him about . . ."—she thought better of that and said instead—"I don't know him well enough to know where he goes when he isn't home."

"Let me guess," Dave said. "You wanted to talk to him about Adam Streeter." Her gaze didn't deny it. He said, "So do I. It was Adam Streeter you did know well enough to know where he went when he wasn't home. Is that it?"

"We were good friends," she said.

"You hadn't quarreled?" Dave said. "That wasn't why he killed himself?"

"Why would anyone quarrel with Adam?" she said. "No. He brought me to this country from Cambodia, and set me on my feet. I would never quarrel with Adam. I don't know why he killed himself. I can't believe he did. He was brave. And he loved being alive." She found tissues in her straw bag and dried her eyes. "Excuse me."

"If you wanted to talk about him," Dave said, "why pick Underhill? Why not Chrissie?"

"He didn't want me to go there," she said. "He didn't want Chrissie to know about me—about us. Or anyone. He was afraid his wife would go to court about it and take Chrissie away from him. And she wasn't a good mother. She had many problems; drink, drugs."

"I know. But she's got Chrissie now."

A wince flickered in the young woman's smooth face. "Ah, he would hate that. It's another reason he wouldn't have killed himself. He wouldn't abandon Chrissie that way. Not so young and helpless." She pinched her nose with the tissues, wadded them in her fist, pushed them back into the straw bag. "Who are you?"

"Dave Brandstetter." He slipped a card from his wallet and gave it to her. She read it, and looked up at him.

"Private investigator?" Her mouth fought back a smile. "There really are such people, then? Not just on television?"

"This one only investigates death claims for insurance companies," Dave said. "When the death is sudden and violent. Did he own a .357 Magnum automatic pistol?"

"He owned a gun," she said, "a handgun. But I think he told me it was"—she frowned and bunked—"what is the name? Something about a horse? A very old American name?"

"Colt?" Dave said. "Why did he keep it?"

"He went dangerous places," she said.

"They wouldn't let him take it on airplanes," Dave said. "Did they let him take you?"

She shook her head. "There were difficulties about my passport. I am not yet an American citizen." She watched the street, the cars pulling away. "I wish Mike would come home."

"Streeter was going to Central America," Dave said. "Would your passport let you go there?"

"He was?" She tilted her head, mouth a little open in surprise. "He never said so to me. When?"

"He had his bags half packed. You mean you didn't know about the story he was working on? About the troubles in Los Inocentes? The guerrilla war?"

She shook her head and said nothing.

"So why have you come to see Underhill?"

"He was Adam's associate. I am alone now, suddenly, without Adam. I have a shop that he bought for me. Flowers." It was her turn to find a business card and hand it to Dave. It was prettier than his, printed in colors. "In Santa Monica. But it doesn't always pay its own way, and he helped. I don't know what will happen now. I have a new delivery van to pay for. I thought Adam might have said something to Mike about me. Maybe Adam made a will. He never mentioned it to me, but if there is a lawyer, perhaps Mike knows his name."

"I'll ask him." Dave pushed her card into his wallet. "Then you won't have to wait for him. I have to see him, anyway. You can go back to your flower shop."

"Thank you," she said. "Will you do that?"

"I promise." Dave smiled. She returned the smile, made a little shy, suddenly, when she had been anything but shy until now. Something had changed between them. Or she thought so. He said, "How do you know so much about Hunsinger?"

"I lived in the rear house for a while," she said, "but Adam didn't like the neighborhood. I was trying not to spend his money foolishly. But he made me move. That's how I know Hunsinger. He's a good man, but he's wasting his time." She smiled again. "Well, goodbye for now, Mr. Brandstetter. And thank you." She stepped away from him, walking backward, the straw bag held in front of her at her knees, little-girlish. At the wide driveway gate, she turned. A padlock fastened this gate, too. She unlocked it, edged out, closed the gate again, the padlock. Aware of him watching her, she said, "I forgot to return the key when I moved." She dropped the keys into the bag, turned to the shiny lavender van parked across the driveway, and reached for its door. "Goodbye."

"Wait." Dave went to the driveway gate. "If you kept a key for this, you kept the key to the rear house, too. Did you go inside, just now?"

She studied him, surprised. "You are like the ones on the television, after all, aren't you? Yes, I kept them. Yes, I went inside. I wondered why he hadn't answered his phone all day. I thought he might be ill."

"Or dead?" Dave said. "Like Adam?"

She didn't answer that. She didn't blink, either, or show any expression. She said, "I left him a note." A hint of smile played at the corners of her mouth. "You'll find it when you go inside. You're going to do that, aren't you? Just like on television?"

"I don't know why so much is missing from Streeter's workroom," Dave said. "Manuscripts, notes, computer storage disks, cassettes. I want to find them. Chrissie thinks Underhill may have them. What do you think?"

"I think someone killed Adam," she said. "Don't you?" She came back to the gate, rummaging in the straw bag. She took out her key packet and pried one key off its hanger. "This may make it easier for you"—she laid the key gravely in his outstretched palm—"to find out who it was."

The house seemed to have saved up stillness. Dave stepped inside and shut the door. The dog had gone through the front house, barking from a series of windows as Dave walked down the driveway. It ended up at the smeared glass of a back door. But its barks came only faintly to the rear house now. Beige wall-to-wall carpet lay under plain upholstered pieces from a bargain department store, plaid couch and two matching chairs in greenish brown, a coffee table, books stacked on it. A pair of brick-red pottery lamps with drum shades waited on end tables. A thirteen-inch television set rested on a low cart in front of a shallow fake fireplace. Stereo speakers and a compact receiver perched on built-in bookcases that divided this room from a dining room that Underhill used as an office.

A sand-color IBM Selectric sat on the table, Fleur's card stuck into it, *Please call me* written on the back. Around the machine lay typed pages, handwritten notes, file cards, photographs, clippings, magazines and books open and shut, pencils, pens, a box of typing paper, a little bottle of Wite-Out. Dave peered through reading glasses at the typing, notes, clippings. All concerned a young woman who acted in a daytime television serial and now was about to star in a motion picture.

No mention of Los Inocentes. Cardboard cartons on the floor against a wall held more papers, notes, clippings. He crouched and poked around in these. The clippings all dealt with show business—except one. HIGHER REWARDS SOUGHT TO CURB TERRORISM. *President Backs Paying Up to $500,000 to Halt Acts Around World.* He folded this, tucked it into a pocket. A slip of paper caught his eye. *Rafael,* and a telephone number. He used Underhill's phone to ring Ray Lollard. A lifelong friend and top telephone company executive, Ray lived in a restored Adams Boulevard mansion, collected costly antiques, and kept a wild-haired, barefoot potter named Kovaks in a renovated stable-studio out back. Dave told Ray he needed a location on the telephone number after Rafael's name. "And why don't you come over next Thursday?" he added. Kovaks was no one to take to a restaurant. He wasn't a drunk, but he favored marijuana, and even when he didn't, he was apt to take a notion in the middle of a meal that he was too warm and strip. It didn't faze Lollard, or Dave either, but it could disconcert strangers. Even Max. "We'll have drinks and dinner and you can meet Cecil. You've never met Cecil, right?"

"I know I'd love him, but I'm not eating these days."

"You were never overweight," Dave said.

"Kovaks has a new helper who weighs a hundred twenty-eight pounds. I am determined to weigh a hundred twenty-eight pounds, darling, if it kills me."

"Ray, you're six feet tall," Dave said. "How big is this clay-smeared elf?"

"He comes up to Kovaks's armpit," Lollard said. "It's irrelevant. Thin I can get. Short—never." He gave a small, tremulous falsetto cry of woe. "Not to worry. I'll locate that telephone for you. It's south, where the big produce ranches are. Don't tell me illegals are buying insurance these days."

"No, but they're dying, just the same," Dave said. "Oh, and Ray, get me an up-to-date phone bill for Adam Streeter, okay?" He gave Lollard the address. "I need to know if he rang that number. And think about Thursday, will you?"

"How can I help it?" Lollard said. "It involves food."

Dave laughed, hung up, and pushed a swing door to Underhill's kitchen. In the sink lay a dinner plate, salad plate, one each of knife, fork, spoon, a coffee mug, a drinking glass. The stove held a coffee maker, empty. On a counter lay a flat pack of bacon, a wrapped stick of butter, two eggs. He put these into the refrigerator. He left the kitchen.

The single window of the bedroom looked out at a fence leaned on by lantana, flowers of calico red and yellow. The bed was unmade, an open book lying on it, reading glasses lying on the book. Pajamas on the floor, corduroy slippers. Under a brass lamp, behind a clock radio on a nightstand were stacked four books, jackets faded and chipped around the edges. Biographies of celebrities. By Michael Underhill. Dave eyed them. He seemed to remember that they, too, were short on facts.

Sweaters, shirts, underwear, socks lay neatly in drawers. Slacks and jackets hung clean and cared for in a closet. The loafers, Hush Puppies, sandals on the floor were in good shape. This was a man down but not out. But a man also not going anywhere: luggage stood dusty on a high shelf. In the small bathroom, a rumpled towel lay across a closed toilet seat. It was damp. The medicine chest held only expected items—razor, shave cream, toothpaste, and the like. No prescription drugs, no illegal drugs. All correct and dull.

A buzzer rasped in the kitchen. Dave left the bathroom and stepped into a short hall. The front door had a big glass panel, but it was bright outside, dark in here. He took off the reading glasses and tucked them away. The man on the stoop was no one he knew. Aged about forty, he had ginger hair, tightly curled, and a sandy moustache. Under a vest of thin leather his T-shirt was stenciled with a biplane, circling it McGregor Flies for Hire. His belly was a little bulgy. The belt buckle there was large and tough-looking, the belt wide and sweat-darkened. This was nobody he had to explain his presence to. He went and opened the door.

"Where the hell have you been?" the man exploded. He gave Dave a push in the chest, barged inside, and slammed the door. "You were supposed to meet me in Escondido at ten thirty this morning. I been phoning and phoning. What happened?"

"My name is Brandstetter," Dave said.

"What?" The man had grown red in the face. Now he turned pale. His voice lost volume. "What are you—a cop?" Dave didn't answer. He gave the man time to look him over. "No. The clothes are wrong. What is that? Brooks Brothers famous summer poplin, right? Three hundred bucks, right? You're no cop. Who are you? Where's Mike Underhill?"

"What was he going to meet you in Escondido about?"

"That's my business," the man said, "and his."

"How can you have business with a man you don't even know?"

"He was a go-between. It was a cash deal. I didn't need to know him. I knew the principal."

"Adam Streeter—right?"

The man's eyes narrowed. "Where do you fit in?"

"Streeter is dead. Shot. He won't be needing that aircraft you were going to sell him. That's what the deal was, wasn't it? Underhill was supposed to bring you the purchase price this morning. Why?"

"The seller needed his money fast. That's why he was letting the plane go so cheap. Shit. What the hell am I going to do now?" He squinted at Dave again. "Shot? Then you are some kind of cop, aren't you? Somebody killed him."

"Possibly," Dave said. "I'm an insurance investigator. And you're McGregor." He nodded at the T-shirt. "That says you fly planes. It doesn't say you sell them."

"These days, every asshole with too much money, too many cars, boats, houses buys a plane. And once they learn, they fly it a few times and then it sits there. They're like kids—don't know what they want. Sometimes I can persuade one of them to get rid of the damned thing. I hate to see a beautiful flying machine sit on the ground. It makes me sick."

"Only this one's going cheap, you said. What kind is it? His daughter says Streeter wanted to fly to faraway places with strange-sounding names."

"He was a foreign correspondent," McGregor said. "It's a Cessna 404 twin engine. No, it wouldn't fly around the bloody world, but he was only going to Tegucigalpa."

"It's a model popular with drug smugglers," Dave said.

McGregor's face got red again. "I don't know why the owner wants to unload it. I don't ask a lot of questions."

"It's a way of covering your ass," Dave said. "Selling hot aircraft could get you into trouble. A hundred thousand?"

McGregor turned for the door. "Yeah, well. It's zilch, now, isn't it?"

"Cash, right?" Dave said. "Drug dealers prefer cash—so they tell me on the five o'clock news."

McGregor opened the door, turned back. "Look, I was only in this like Underhill was. A go-between, understand? A broker. It was nothing to do with me."

"It's a lot of money," Dave said, "and a man is dead."

"I was way the hell down the coast. Why would I kill him, anyway? I liked the man. We met in Nam. I flew supply helicopters. Afterward, when he was in a rush, he'd have me fly him places. Also teach him to fly. Then he threw this deal my way. He was money in the bank. Why would I kill him? You start worrying about that hundred thousand. Where is it?" He laughed sourly. "Same place as Mike Underhill, right?"

"It looks that way," Dave said.

But he couldn't locate him. Using Underhill's telephone, he rang every number in the man's thin, leather-covered book. But no one who answered had seen Underhill in days.

## 4

DAVE MADE HIS way through a wide, brightly lighted room where detectives laughed and swore, typewriters rattled, telephones rang. They sat on steel chairs at steel desks among file cabinets and dealt with the phones and the paperwork and tried to feed themselves—Dave smelled pizzas, burritos, tuna salad sandwiches. He found a passageway that led between small boxy offices, half paneled, half glass, to a door at the end marked CAPT. KENNETH R. BARKER. Inside, a woman officer, not in uniform, in a strict, shirtwaist dress, sorted manila folders until the door clicked behind Dave, when she peered up at him over reading glasses that made her look like a small girl playing grandma.

"Dave Brandstetter," Dave said. "Is he in?"

She read her watch, frowned. "He's just going home."

"He'll see me," Dave said. He and Ken Barker went back thirty years, at least. They'd often butted heads. But this had slowly, grudgingly established respect in each man for the other. They'd met when Barker was still a plain detective. Years and work had made him a lieutenant.

Now in his sixties, he was a captain. His hair had gone from solid black to pure white. The inner door opened and he bulked in it now, shoulders straining the seams of his shirt, which was, as usual, open at the collar, the knot of his tie pulled down. His nose had been broken long ago, flattened. Heavy brow ridges helped make him look like a boxer. Under them his eyes were gray. He smiled.

"You caught me just in time. I'm off to London for a conference tomorrow. Come in." He waved a thick hand. Dave went past him into the inner office. Barker said, "Tell anyone who calls I've already left." He closed the door.

Dave said, "Your man Leppard neglected to put into his report on the Adam Streeter death that he'd confiscated the victim's papers, computer storage disks, cassettes."

"The writer? Down at the marina?" Barker sat down.

"I found only old stuff," Dave said. "His daughter told me he was working on a hot story about Los Inocentes. There's nothing there. Not even a note." Barker nodded at a chair and Dave took it. Day was dying outside the wide vertical steel strips that were blinds on the windows. The place was called the glass house. Until the blinds went up, all that glass made it too hot. Lord, how long ago that was. "He was an active and successful writer. There should have been papers. I'd like to look at them."

"Just a minute," Barker said, "I'll check." He worked a telephone on his desk, murmured instructions into it, and hung up the receiver. "You're on this for which insurance company? Not Medallion."

"Somehow," Dave said, "they never think of me. No, it's Banner. Otis Lovejoy. I wish I had a secretary."

"What about that youngster, Harris?" Barker said.

"You saw his bullet scars," Dave said. "He's gone back to television news. If you look sharp, you may see him."

Barker nodded. "I have." He got out of his chair. Not with the spring of thick muscle he used to possess. Heavily.

He opened a cabinet of burled wood. Inside stood bottles and glasses. "Martini?" He didn't turn to see if Dave nodded. He bent to the bottom section of the cabinet and found ice cubes there. "Just the other night." Barker dropped ice cubes into glasses. "That shooting in San Feliz—the young Latino with no ID. Your kid was right on top of it. He knows how to ask questions." Barker came with Dave's drink, set his own on the desk, went back and folded shut the glossy cabinet doors. He sat behind the desk, lifted his glass, gave Dave a tight little grin. "I wonder where he learned that."

Dave twitched him a smile. "I wonder," he said.

The phone rang and Barker picked it up. He listened and frowned. He listened some more, grunted, hung up the receiver. "Leppard didn't find any papers. Just like you."

"Is he looking for them?" Dave said. "I think the papers are what got Streeter killed. Find the papers, find the killer. Leppard doesn't strike me as wide awake."

"He was this morning," Barker said. "He arrested the killer. A writer called Mike Underhill."

"Did Underhill have the papers?" Dave said.

"No, but he had something better—a hundred thousand dollars in cash. Streeter's money from a deal he'd struck with a television producer. Leppard got confirmation of that from Streeter's bank."

"It was to buy a Cessna 404 from a man named McGregor."

Barker cocked an admiring eyebrow above his glass. "You've been getting around. But that's a scam. Underhill is famous for scams. And McGregor is shadier than he is. McGregor doesn't sell aircraft. He flies hot television sets and dirty money south, and drugs and brown babies north. He's well known to us."

Dave stared. "Brown babies?"

"Mexican newborns," Barker said. "To childless couples. Five thousand dollars the mortal soul. It's not big in California yet. It's mostly a Texas racket."

"Dear God." Dave tasted his martini. It was bottled, premixed, not very good. "I don't think Streeter was into smuggling. He liked danger, but a different kind."

"What he was into isn't the point," Barker said. "The point is, what was Underhill into. You know what Leppard found lying right beside his typewriter? An airline ticket. One way. To North Africa somewhere. Algiers? Algiers."

"It doesn't prove murder," Dave said. "There's a guard on the gate at Streeter's place. Did Underhill visit him at three in the morning? Did Leppard ask the guard?"

Barker nodded. "He asked, and the guard said only tenants came. And nobody late. But sea air makes you sleepy. The guard could have nodded. Underhill could have reached in and worked the switch to open the gates."

Dave lifted and dropped a hand. "Whoever killed Streeter didn't come in that way. They came in off the balcony to Streeter's workroom. Third floor. Don't ask me how they got there—from the roof, I suppose. They knocked over two flowerpots on their way. I saw the flowerpots."

Barker sat still. "Did Leppard see them?"

"I'll ask him when I see him. I want to see him."

Barker read his watch. "Tomorrow."

Dave tasted his drink—it was no better this time. "And one more favor, if I may," he said. "The registration on a late-model white BMW." He recited the license number on the car of the woman who had argued about the cat with De Lis at the condominium gates this morning.

Barker penciled the numbers on a pad, picked up the phone, murmured instructions and read the numbers into it, and hung up. He downed another gulp of whiskey and grinned at Dave. "You're right," he said. "A secretary is a wonderful thing."

Hilda Vosper, a gray but chipper widow who lived just up the trail, appeared in the Jaguar's headlights. She wore jeans, sneakers, a boy's windbreaker jacket, and was walking her ragged little dog. Dave braked to say a neighborly hello. The dog barked and jumped like a fur yo-yo. Hilda Vosper laughed and waved a small friendly hand, and Dave jounced down into the yard of the converted stables where he lived. The front building was dark. Of course. Cecil's van wasn't here. No one was home. Dave locked the Jaguar, and rounded the raw-shingled end of the building to a courtyard sheltered by a big old live oak. He was used to the roughness of the weathered brick paving, but it jarred him tonight. Jumping that fence had been a mistake. He ached.

He unlocked the heavy door of the front building, stepped onto deep carpet, touched a switch so that lamplight made warm circles in the vast, raftered room with its several levels, several groupings of comfortable—he hated coming home to an empty house. He'd never lived alone. First, he'd lived with his father and a succession of beautiful stepmothers—until the Army took him. After the war, he'd lived with Rod Fleming for twenty-two years, until Rod died of cancer. Then there'd been Doug Sawyer, a nice man but one who needed somebody Dave was not. And now there was Cecil Harris, a young black newsman he'd met on a case four or five years ago, up the coast.

Driving here from Parker Center, feeling tired, Dave had hoped Cecil would get time off for dinner tonight. He was working two shifts this week. Dave was missing him badly, and it was only Wednesday. He stepped behind a bar at the near end of the room and built himself a double martini. He switched on sound equipment, and violins, viola, cello sang from a compact disc—the Haydn opus 20, number 5 quartet. He sat down, pried off his shoes, and with a sigh stretched out on a couch to drink his martini, smoke a cigarette, and listen. And the telephone rang. Of course. He stretched an arm for it.

"I've been trying to reach you all day." It was Otis Lovejoy at Banner Insurance, a sleek black executive with sad eyes. "You should get an answering machine."

"I have one, but I hate the damn things, don't you?"

"It's about the Streeter death," Lovejoy said. "They've got the killer. A man who worked for Streeter."

"Mike Underhill," Dave said. "I know, but—"

"He had a hundred thousand dollars of Streeter's money, and he was about to fly to Algeria with it."

"So why hadn't he packed?" Dave said. "His grips are in his bedroom closet, covered with dust."

"You were at his place?" Lovejoy chuckled. "I'm always amazed at how fast you work."

"I thought he'd have Streeter's papers. They're missing. They shouldn't be missing, Otis. Whoever killed him took his papers. Underhill didn't have them, so it wasn't Underhill."

"What kind of papers?" Lovejoy said.

Dave told him. He finished, "The story was so dangerous he didn't want his daughter to know about it. It was so dangerous it killed him. That's what kind of papers."

"Forget it," Lovejoy said. "All we needed to know was that he didn't kill himself. He met death at the hands of another. And the other was not the beneficiary. I've already approved payment on the policy to his daughter."

"Don't send the check," Dave said. "Make up excuses. If you send it now, the mother will spend it on booze."

"All right if I send you your check?" Lovejoy said.

"All donations gratefully received," Dave said, and rattled the receiver into place. And Cecil came in, smiling. Dave smiled back. "I was hoping for this." He started to get up. "A drink?"

"I'll get it." Cecil went behind the bar and bent his long, lean self over the small refrigerator there. He came bearing a frosty green Heineken bottle and a glass. "Whew." He plumped down on the couch, and tilted the bottle so the beer piled up foam in the glass. "They are working my black butt off at that place."

"God forbid." Dave leaned up and gave him a quick kiss. "Do you have to go back tonight? You look used up."

"I'm on call, all right? Till ten thirty. And until ten thirty, I am very likely to sleep."

Dave knocked back his martini and rose, pushing feet into shoes. "I'll fix you something to eat, first."

Cecil caught his belt and pulled him back down. "Relax. No need to cook. Supper's in the cookshack, the warming oven. I stopped at Max's on my way home." He meant Max Romano's restaurant, Dave's favorite haunt. Cecil set glass and bottle on a coffee table among fancifully painted Mexican pottery owls and cats. He went to the bar with Dave's glass. "I figured you'd be tired, too, up half the night typing that report for Goldring, then starting a new case today." His hands worked in the shadows with gin, vermouth, and ice that jingled cheerfully in a Swedish crystal pitcher. "How does that one look?"

"It looks all wrong." Dave told Cecil about it. Halfway through, Cecil brought him an icy glass and set it in his hand. He dropped onto the couch and slumped there, long legs stretched out, sipping at his beer, and listening while Haydn sweetened the background. Dave finished, "But whatever it was, it wasn't suicide, and so I'm off it."

Cecil got up and went for another Heineken, saying, "Streeter was at my workplace the night he was killed."

Dave sat up straight. "You're not serious."

"You remember how late I got home? Working on that killing down in San Feliz?"

"Three o'clock," Dave said. He'd been unable to sleep for worry, had kept waking every ten minutes to reach for the clock with its red glowing numerals, wondering if Cecil had been right, after all, to go back to the news business. Working with Dave had once got him shot almost to death. Working with Dave had put a gun in his hand and forced him to kill a man. But was the news business any safer? Where the hell was he, anyway? In the dark, Dave had pawed out for the telephone, then drawn back his hand. He was going to make a fool of himself, and of Cecil, which was worse. Instead, he got out of bed, went down the raw wooden steps from the raw wooden sleeping loft in the rear building, poured Glenlivet over ice cubes in a thick glass, and found a book to read. He stretched out on the corduroy couch in solitary lamplight, listened for the sound of Cecil's van, and told himself grumpily not to be a mother hen. "You got to the studio at one and then you had to edit the film. Unidentified young Latino, face down in the water of an irrigation canal, shot through the head."

"Nobody knew him," Cecil said. "Nobody ever saw him before. Everybody muttered and crossed themselves a lot and rolled their eyes. Some of them were throwing kids and chickens into pickup trucks and leaving before I could start asking questions. Weird scene. You could smell the fear in the air. Sharper than chili peppers."

Dave tasted his drink. "You make a mean martini."

But Cecil was brooding. "They're never going to find out who did that. He's just dead meat. Not even a name to put on his grave. Wasn't any older than I am. Where did he come from? He had to be staying in one of those shacky little so-called houses with all those old people, pregnant girls, kids, young men looking fifty. But no one knew him, not a stoop laborer, not a foreman, not a rancher."

"They knew him," Dave said. "They just didn't want trouble with Immigration and Naturalization. Tell me about Streeter. What did he want at your television station?"

"A talk with the news director. Urgently."

"Donaldson—is that his name?"

Cecil nodded. "Who does not work that shift, right? And Jimmie Caesar and Dot Yamada said, tell us, but he wouldn't tell them. I was busy. I'd just gone along the hall to the men's room. That was how I happened to see him. Doors are half glass there. He was loud, agitated. Door was closed, but it didn't stop the sound. He was saying just what his daughter told you."

"That he had the hottest story of the decade?" Dave said. "That surprises me. Did they find Donaldson?"

"They were scared to try." Cecil took a fast gulp of beer. "He's a bear. And he's got a wife and five kids, but he sleeps around, tells her he's at the station when he's really bedding down some pretty new lady, all right? So they didn't want to phone. Couldn't very well explain that to Streeter, could they? Seeing their faces, I couldn't help but laugh."

"But they knew who Streeter was, surely," Dave said. "A Pulitzer Prize winner? They had to take him seriously."

"If they didn't know before," Cecil said. "They knew it after he got a sore throat yelling at them. He was—how shall I put it—just a little bit keyed up."

"Not frightened?" Dave wondered.

"Frightened?" Turning the word over in his mind, Cecil sat forward, tilted the remaining beer from the green bottle into his glass, piling up the foam again. The Haydn strings traced lacy patterns in the canyon stillness. "Maybe." He looked hard at Dave. "What makes you think so?"

"He was a print journalist, not a broadcaster." Dave's jacket lay over the couch arm. He rummaged in it for cigarettes. "He stood to make a lot of money and build his reputation with a story on paper—for the *New York Times,* the *Washington Post,* some place like that. Yet here he is, suddenly ready to rush the story out on television." He clicked a slim steel lighter to set his cigarette going. "Also, he dashed home and started to pack. Someone was after him, and he was running scared. That's what it looks like."

"Not so scared he was giving the story to hired hands," Cecil said. "It had to be the head honcho or nobody. So finally Dot Yamada picked up the phone and rang for Donaldson. He'd never forgive Jimmie, but maybe he'd forgive a pretty lady."

"And Donaldson was home in his own bed for once?"

"Strange as it seems," Cecil said.

"And he agreed to come?" Dave sipped the icy martini.

"Lives in Malibu. Agreed to meet Streeter at his condominium. That would be quickest."

"You're sure?" Dave said.

"I read Dot's lips when she hung up the phone," Cecil said. "It was plain as could be. 'He'll meet you at your house,' she said, and smiled."

"Only he didn't, did he?" Dave said. "Chrissie would have heard him. And she didn't hear him. Streeter was the only one she heard come home that night—no one else."

"Jesus," Cecil said. "What you're saying is Dot's phone call was a fake. She only pretended to talk to Donaldson. She was stringing Streeter along."

"If Donaldson had gone," Dave said, "he'd have had a scoop on the murder, wouldn't he? It would have been all over your store. All over the newscasts. And it wasn't."

"Shit." Cecil shook his head glumly. "Dot Yamada sent him home to be killed. She was playing a game."

"She couldn't have known," Dave said, "but it wasn't the way to handle it." He got to his feet. "We'd better eat. Food can dry out in warming ovens." He watched Cecil gather up beer bottle and glass, and take them to the shadowy bar. Dave moved toward the door. "What did Max send?"

Cecil said, "It's those veal scallops he does with the melted Swiss cheese and all." He followed Dave out into the coolness of the night, crickets singing down the dark canyon. He pulled the door shut behind him, and they crossed the bumpy brick courtyard, curled oak leaves crackling under their feet.

Dave said, "You know all about current events."

Cecil shrugged. *"Poquito,"* he said.

"Then tell me, please"—Dave paused for a last intake from his cigarette before he flicked it away, sparking red across the bricks—"about one Cortez-Ortiz."

"General Cortez-Ortiz." Cecil stepped around Dave and opened the cookshack door. The light inside was cheerful. The aroma of Max's cooking was rich in the air. Cecil said, "I'll tell you while we eat."

## 5

WHEN DAVE'S FATHER died of a heart attack, four or five years ago, while racing his new Bentley along a midnight freeway, he had widowed his ninth wife, a smart, good-looking, very young woman named Amanda. She had wandered dolefully through the enormous rooms of Carl Brandstetter's showy Beverly Hills house, wondering what to do with her life, until Dave talked her into remodeling this place for him. Lately she'd added a second sleeping loft in the rear building—this after a case Dave worked on had meant housing a family of children with no place else to hide. Added sleeping quarters seemed sensible. Now he had them. The back building still held the tang of freshly sawed lumber. But the cookshack Amanda had done on the first go-round. It stood at the near side of the brick courtyard, about twelve by fifteen feet, shingled like the two larger buildings. Those she had modernized— temperately. This one she had turned backward in time. Walls and cupboards she'd stripped to the original pine. The refrigerator-freezer was new in its works, but housed in a gigantic old oaken icebox of many thick doors. The cookstove was a stately farmhouse model of white porcelain panels framed by glittering nickel plate, cunningly fitted out with the latest burners, grille, rotisserie, convection oven. The sink came from a wrecker's, but was unmarred. Beside it stood a cast-iron hand pump. Amanda's workmen had uncovered plumbing beneath the building that reached down to a well. The pump now worked, but there were faucets, too. To eat their supper, Cecil and Dave sat on plain pine chairs at a heavy old deal table scoured almost white. Cecil said:

"He was minister of the interior in Los Inocentes. Under the old military junta. And under the new *presidente*, too, after they held those so-called elections so the U.S. would loan them money. But Washington held back on the loans after reporters got down there and proved the guerrillas were right—that El Carnicero was still slaughtering *campesinos* in the back country—whole villages of them."

"El Carnicero—the Butcher." Dave drank wine from a chilled, misty glass. "That's Cortez-Ortiz?"

"Believe it." Cecil filled his mouth, chewed, swallowed, drank some wine. "Some congressmen got on a plane and went down to see for themselves. And there were the corpses by the roads, in the ditches, in the fields, in the town squares, and they told the State Department they wouldn't authorize any money for the new democratic Los Inocentes until El Presidente got rid of the Butcher. Cortez-Ortiz had his own army, paid with government funds. Elite troops, all right? Only nobody calls them that. They call them *chuchos*."

"What kind of Spanish is that?" Dave said.

Cecil shrugged. "I don't know. It means 'little dogs.'"

"And what happened to the Butcher and his little dogs?"

"He got sent into exile." Cecil wolfed down another forkful of Max's special scallopini and followed it with another swallow of wine. "Not far—only to Honduras, the Guatemalan embassy. The leftists want him tried for genocide. The rightists want him back as interior minister. But El Presidente—he just wants that juicy U.S. loan."

"Did he disband the special troops?" Dave said.

"With a lot of fanfare. But only for the media. They're still out there murdering people. And disappearing people."

"That didn't used to be a transitive verb," Dave said.

"It's transitive now—one way, no return." Cecil picked up a slim green bottle, poured wine from it into Dave's glass, into his. "And not just *indios* and *mestizos,* either. They did it to a young *yanqui* reporter the other day. Twenty-four hours in Los Inocentes. They found his jeep in the mountains. Then they found his body, bullet in the back of his head."

"Rue Glendenning," Dave said. "His name came up this morning. I wondered where I'd heard it before. On the news. He came to Streeter for advice on launching a career."

"Must have been some advice," Cecil said bleakly. "State Department lodged a protest. El Presidente was saddened, but he says the guerrillas did it. The communists, no? *Sí.*" Cecil moved his head sharply, as if to shake off the memory. He made himself smile. "It's nice being here with you," he said.

"It's not exactly an everyday occurrence anymore," Dave said. He glanced at a yellow telephone fixed to the end of a cupboard where it could be reached from the table. "I hope they don't call you."

"What will we do to pass the time?" Cecil wondered.

"We'll think of something." Dave finished his food, brooding, puzzling. He rose, gathered up the dishes, carried them to the sink. Coffee was ready on the massive stove, steam curling light and fragrant from a glass maker. He lifted down from a shelf handsome mugs glazed in runny brown, filled these, carried them to the table. Bottles sat glistening on a counter. He lifted from among them a squat one, turned a squeaky cork, poured brandy into small globe glasses, returned to the table with these, and sat down.

"Who brought up Cortez-Ortiz, anyway?" Cecil said.

"His name was one of two things Streeter's daughter knew about the story her father was working on. That's all she'd heard from him. Overheard when he was talking to Glendenning. Two names. The other was Tegucigalpa."

"That figures," Cecil said. He picked up his coffee mug, blew at it, set it down again. "Four or five days ago, there was some wild shooting at the Guatemalan consulate in Tegucigalpa. When the smoke cleared, and they dragged the bodies off the steps and washed the blood away, Cortez-Ortiz was nowhere to be found."

Dave looked at him over his raised mug. "Disappeared?"

"You got it. And no one knows who shot his guards and took him. Left-wing? Right-wing? All the confusion out front, somebody snatched him out the back."

"And what Streeter learned on that long drive of his was who," Dave said. "Only he was seen. Someone was watching and knew Streeter had the truth. And Streeter knew he knew. Which was why he ran to television. If the story became public right away, there'd be no point in killing him to keep him quiet."

Cecil sipped cautiously at the hot coffee, frowning to himself. He set the mug down. "But he shouldn't have fallen for Dot's story about Donaldson. He should have stayed at the television station where there were people around, where he'd be safe."

Dave shrugged. "He was packing to clear out when they caught up to him. He was using the time."

Cecil said bleakly, "Only he'd figured on more time than he had." He picked up his little globe of brandy. "He should just have given the story to Jimmie and Dot." He tilted and revolved the snifter slowly, watching the amber fluid slide, clinging to the glass. "What story could be so big it's worth getting killed for? What amount of money and fame?" He sipped from the glass. "Mmm. If there is one thing in this world as good as sex, it's brandy."

"We'll see," Dave said. "Somebody knows what Streeter knew. Nothing on Cortez-Ortiz on the news wires?"

"Only that he's still missing," Cecil said. "Didn't take but a minute for the pretty talking heads on the anchor desk to say that, and get along to the baseball scores and other really important stuff, did it?"

"It doesn't make sense." Dave tasted the coffee, the brandy, and the flavors needed tobacco smoke to perfect the blend. He lit a cigarette. "Why kidnap the man, if you don't ask for ransom—or at least brag about it?"

"I don't know." Cecil watched Dave smoke, and frowned. "Why can't you quit that? I'd like you around for a while."

"I'm down to a pack a day," Dave said.

"The Grim Reaper will be furious," Cecil said.

Some kind of rattly vehicle jounced down the sharp drop from the road to the parking space beyond the front building. Dave kept meaning to have that access fixed—his Jaguar sometimes scraped bottom there. Now he was pleased that he'd left it. It gave advance warning of visitors. He laid his napkin down, pushed back his chair, went to the door that stood open to the night, pushed the screen, and looked out. Silhouetted by the glow of lights that crouched in the shrubbery out front, a lanky man came walking bowlegged over the bricks. He wore a cowboy hat. Dave found a switch and lights came on under the eaves of the buildings, putting light in the courtyard. The man was very fair—white skin, white eyebrows, white eyelashes. He blinked in the sudden light, halted, and studied Dave.

"Brandstetter? I heard you wanted to talk to me."

"Did I?" Dave said. "I don't remember that."

"My dog remembers," the man said, straight-faced, no hint of mockery in his voice. "He told me you came by my house this afternoon, knocking at the door. He takes messages—but you didn't have any way of knowing that, did you?"

"Hunsinger," Dave said. "Come in."

Hunsinger came in. He had a droopy white frontier moustache. His white hair was long, tied in a ponytail with a strip of blue cloth. His Levi pants and jacket were old, the blue almost leached out of them. The heels of his cowboy boots were run over. His blue tanktop had holes in it. Cecil shut the dishwasher and the pine doors that concealed it, dried his hands, shook Hunsinger's hand. The two of them sat at the table while Dave fetched three mugs of coffee and sat down.

"I don't doubt what you say about the dog," he said, "but I think it was Fleur who told you about me. And not that I wanted to see you. I went to your door by mistake."

"That's all right, if you believe in mistakes." Hunsinger almost smiled. His eyes were a very pale blue. He took off the cowboy hat, glanced around, saw the row of shiny brass hangers by the door, lofted the hat in that direction with the offhandedness of total confidence. It covered a hanger and stayed. Cecil applauded. Hunsinger said to Dave, "I don't believe in mistakes. My observation is that whatever people do, there's a reason for it, whether they know it or not. There are no accidents. There are no mistakes."

"And that's how you help addicts," Dave said.

Hunsinger said, "Getting people to recognize that what they do they always do for a reason is not easy."

"Fleur says you're a nice man, but wasting your time."

"That's funny, coming from her. Where would she be now if somebody hadn't helped her? Has she forgotten?"

"I don't think so," Dave said. "But maybe she doesn't make the association."

"We all need help occasionally," Hunsinger said. "Adam Streeter helped her. I help my junkies. When they let me." He shrugged bony shoulders, slurped some coffee. "I've had a couple successes. Or they have. Anyway, it's more useful than teaching basic psychology in a community college— which is what I did. To a bunch of kids ninety percent of whom can barely write their own names. That's a shuck."

"What about basketball?" Cecil said. "Weren't they after you with scholarships? They were after me, and I can't shoot the way you shot that hat."

Hunsinger almost smiled again. "They were after me, but so was the army. The scholarships dried up while I was in Nam. But basketball doesn't help anybody, either. I had to get out on the streets. That's where people are hurting."

"So I really did want to see you?" Dave said.

"I'm sitting here at your kitchen table," Hunsinger said.

"Put me in touch"—Dave smiled—"with my hidden motives. Why do I want to see you?"

"Because you want to know who killed Adam Streeter."

Dave reached for the cigarette pack, which lay on the table with his lighter. Cecil was quicker. He put his hand over them. Dave sighed. He told Hunsinger, "I did. But it isn't my business anymore. The insurance company that hired me has closed the investigation."

"Because Underhill killed him?" Hunsinger said. "Well, I don't think Underhill killed him." The pale eyes searched Dave's face. There was great gentleness in those eyes. In another age, Hunsinger would have been a priest, and probably a martyr. "Do you want to know why?"

"It's Banner Insurance that's lost interest," Dave said. "Not I." He stood up. "Brandy with that coffee?"

Hunsinger shook his head. Dave went to get brandy for Cecil and himself, and Hunsinger talked. "I don't sleep much. After I gave up booze and cigarettes, I found I didn't need to. At first, I didn't understand, and I worried. But it was all right. Now I can read, plenty of time for it, not too many interruptions. I get twice the work done I used to. Read and write. Daytimes, it's people, okay? So, I was awake and I heard somebody passing under my bedroom window."

"Didn't the dog hear them first?" Dave set the little snifters on the table and sat down. "He raved at me."

"He doesn't bark when I'm there," Hunsinger said. "His ears were up. He heard them all right. My light was on, but the blinds were closed. I switched off the light and opened the blinds. But I didn't see them. Light's bad out there at two in the morning. Trees, shrubs, vines. They'd gone on past— gone on toward the back, toward Underhill's house."

"Was he home?" Dave said.

"His car was out front on the street," Hunsinger said. "Street's always parked up. It was a few doors along. A big old Cougar he paid about two hundred dollars for when he got out of jail. He had to be home. It was after the bars close. Where would he be? See, I went out the front door. I mean—I didn't want to confront whoever was sneaking around. But I wanted a look at them if I could get it."

"Why didn't you phone the police?" Cecil said.

Hunsinger's mournful horse face pitied Cecil's ignorance. He said patiently, "The police are not my friends. They keep claiming I deal drugs. They don't like the company I keep. They wish I wouldn't bring drunks and addicts to my house. They want me to buy a business license. They want me to move. I leave them alone, in the hope they'll leave me alone."

"Right," Cecil said, "sorry."

"And here," Hunsinger told Dave, "out in the middle of the street with its motor idling is this big four-wheel-drive vehicle up high on its tires, you know? With smoked glass windows. Was somebody inside? I bet on it, but the lights were out in my house so I don't think he saw me. I stepped down and waited in the yard, and it wasn't two minutes before these figures came down the driveway, jumped the gate, climbed into the four-wheel and drove off."

"What kind of figures?" Dave said. "How many?"

"Two," Hunsinger said. "You're not going to believe this. In camouflage suits, combat boots, berets. Disorienting. I thought I was back in Saigon. I thought it was 1969."

"You mean they were Orientals?" Dave said. Hunsinger shook his head. "At a guess, Latinos."

"Did you go check with Underhill?" Cecil said.

"I rang his bell. Nobody came. I used my key. I thought they'd done something to him. Went through the whole house, but he wasn't there."

Cecil said, "That's bad for your idea that Underhill is innocent. It was near that time that Streeter was murdered."

"He wouldn't walk to the marina," Hunsinger said.

"It's possible," Dave said. "It's not all that far."

"Why would he? The Cougar was there. It runs. It burns a hell of a lot of gas, but it runs."

Dave said, "What did the commandos want? Had they searched? Had they taken anything?"

"They'd been inside. Through the bathroom window. The screen was leaning against the wall under it. But nothing was missing—not that I could see. Certainly nothing big. Anything big—I'd have seen them carry it out, right?"

"Underhill was home in the morning," Dave said. He got the cigarette pack this time. Cecil was staring at Hunsinger, absorbed. He didn't even notice. Dave got the lighter and lit a cigarette. He laid the lighter down with a click. "You didn't see him? He didn't say anything?"

"I didn't wake up in time," Hunsinger said. "I go to sleep around sunup and catch three, maybe four hours. The police woke me, running under my window, with rifles, for God's sake, surrounding Underhill's, pounding on his door. I got the hell out of there. I haven't been back." He shifted on the chair, dug from a tight pocket a strapless wristwatch with a scratched crystal. "Have to go back soon, though. Have to feed Snowy, let him out in the yard."

"If they didn't take anything," Cecil said, "then what did they come for? A social call? By the bathroom window?"

"They knew he was out, probably telephoned and lured him out. Maybe he did have the papers. Maybe that was what they took."

Dave looked at Hunsinger. "Were Fleur and Underhill having an affair?"

Hunsinger gaped. "Jesus, you ask funny questions. No. I don't think so. Not at his place. She never came there. And I never saw him at her place."

"The flower shop," Dave said. "You go there often?"

"Pretty often. It's a nursery, too. I help her out with the heavy work." A flush appeared under Hunsinger's very white skin. "Wouldn't you? She's a lovely young lady."

"But she never gave you any encouragement?"

"Streeter was a god to her," Hunsinger said. "I'm a mere mortal. I didn't stand a chance."

Dave smoked for a moment. "What about that Blazer, Bronco, whatever it was—did you get the license number?"

"It was too dark. But one thing I can tell you"—Hunsinger scraped back his chair, rose, tucked the watch away—"there was a pintle mount bolted to the roof."

"Say what?" Cecil looked blank.

"A mount for a medium-weight machine gun." Hunsinger walked to get his hat, the heels of the cowboy boots noisy. "That was a combat-ready vehicle."

"Go to the police," Dave said. Hunsinger winced.

"You want to help Underhill, don't you?" Cecil said.

"That's why I came here." Hunsinger took down his hat and put it on. He said to Dave, "You've got a big reputation. Fleur said you also care about people, and I guess you do." Hunsinger pushed the screen door, stepped out, held the door. "Someone set Underhill up for that murder. He's a creep, but they're worse. Someone has to help him. It can't be me—not the way I stand with the police. They'd laugh at me, if they didn't lock me up." Hunsinger walked away. The screen door wheezed closed on its patent piston. The latch clicked. Hunsinger's voice drifted back out of the darkness. "You help him. Only don't send me a bill, okay? All the mail I ever get is bills."

## 6

Leppard was thirty-five and black, bulky and muscular. White streaked his clipped hair from front to back above his left ear. Someone made his clothes to measure, someone gifted. He stood at his desk, watching Dave uneasily. "I saw the flowerpots," he said. "I saw a lot of things, mostly a dead man on the floor in his own blood, mostly that, and this gun with the silencer on it, and this young blind girl with a coffee stain down the front of her blouse, standing there so quiet she could be dead, too. I forgot about the flowerpots."

"And you also forgot that she hadn't heard anyone come into the house except her father," Dave said.

"Hadn't heard the gun go off, either," Leppard said, and sat down. "Teenagers sleep hard, Mr. Brandstetter. I didn't think it meant much what she heard and didn't hear."

"It did, because whoever killed him came over the roofs, swung down to the balcony, knocking over the flowerpots on his way, and walked in through the open French doors."

"That's television cop-show stuff," Leppard said.

"The guard is no teenager. The guard didn't see Underhill."

"Didn't need to. Underhill could have been in that house waiting all the time. Hours. The girl is blind. No one can verify that he was home or where he was. Why wasn't it him kicked over the flowerpots, leaving afterward?"

"How did you come to arrest him?" Dave said.

"We got a telephone tip," Leppard said. A uniformed officer with blond hair and rosy cheeks came in with mugs of coffee on a brown tray, little envelopes of sugar and powdered creamer, a rattle of white plastic stirring sticks. He set the tray on Leppard's paper-strewn desk and went away, closing the door. "Said Underhill did it for a hundred thousand bills Streeter had lying around, and we better move on him because he was fixing to fly away to Africa and disappear. Sure enough—"

"Sure enough, you found the airline ticket for Algiers," Dave said, "lying right there in plain sight beside his typewriter on the dining room table."

"Sure enough," Leppard said with a smile. He reached across the desk and set one of the steaming mugs close to Dave. "Sugar? Cream?" With beautiful pink nails he tore open little packets and emptied them into his mug. "But mostly, sure enough, we found the hundred thou in a brown envelope. And sure enough, the bank confirmed they had given it to Streeter in exchange for a cashier's check from some TV producer."

Dave fixed his own coffee. "A setup," he said. And told Leppard what Hunsinger had told him. "They didn't break in to steal anything," he finished, and sat down, holding the mug. Pigeons cooed and strutted on the windowsill. He watched them. "They broke in to leave something. That airline ticket."

Leppard took a Dunhill cigarette from a dark red box. He lit it with a Dunhill lighter. Smoke trickled through his smile. He shook his head. "The ticket clerk at the airline counter at LAX saw his picture and gave us a positive ID. The man even showed his passport. Mike Underhill bought that ticket."

Dave tried the coffee. "And his passport was lying there on the table by the typewriter with the ticket—am I right?"

"You're right," Leppard said.

"So a slender man in his forties, five eleven, brown eyes, thinning black hair, and olive skin, flashing Underhill's passport—unnecessary, but so he'd be remembered—bought a ticket to Algiers, climbed through Underhill's window, left both items in his house, and then phoned you to come arrest Underhill."

"Underhill worked for Streeter." Leppard studied Dave across the desk, across the coffee mugs, through the cigarette smoke. "You know associates kill associates far more often than strangers. Who told you about the camouflaged dudes?"

"A witness I'm inclined to believe," Dave said.

"Underhill claims Streeter gave him all that cash to—"

"Buy an aircraft from a man named McGregor down the coast," Dave said. "It's not a bad story. McGregor will confirm it."

"We can't find him," Leppard said. "He's disappeared."

"Which ought to suggest something to you," Dave said. "A boy who lives in a condominium near Streeter's, Dan'l Chapman, told me Streeter was planning to buy a plane."

"He'll make a good witness for Underhill," Leppard said.

"Unless he disappears, too. The couple whose apartment faces Streeter's across the patio with the swimming pool—people name of Gernsbach—they've disappeared. Did you know that? Within hours of the time Streeter was killed. Don't you find that interesting? I do."

Leppard sighed impatiently. "The DA likes Underhill for this, a con man with a record of outsmarting himself."

"A man can be a lot of bad things," Dave said, "and still not be a murderer." He swallowed coffee again, grimaced, set the mug on the desk. "Find Gernsbach, Sergeant. His windows look straight across at the room where Streeter died. Maybe he saw who did it and ran away in fear. Find him."

Leppard's big hand came to rest on a stack of manila file folders on the desk. "With all this to do? We have a lock on Underhill. No need to look further, no time for it."

Dave took a deep breath and told Leppard about Streeter's hot story. "I think he learned the identity of the people who snatched Cortez-Ortiz, and they killed him before he could write it—or broadcast it." He told about Streeter at the television station. "He knew they were after him. That was why he was packing his bags."

"If you were a terrorist"—Leppard delicately scratched his head—"and made that kind of coup, wouldn't you tell the world instead of keeping it secret? Ask for an exchange of prisoners for him? Or money to run your revolution?"

"No one has," Dave said. "That seems to answer that."

"It still doesn't make plausible the idea that Central American terrorists are climbing condominiums at the LA marina and prowling the streets of shacky old Venice beach in combat boots and berets, breaking into bungalows—now does it?"

"Before they broke in," Dave said, "they rang Underhill and asked him to meet them somewhere, didn't they?"

"Down at the fishing pier. That's what he says. But nobody saw him there that we can find. As an alibi, it stinks. He was down at Streeter's, shooting him."

"The Desert Eagle .357 Magnum was his, then?"

Leppard shrugged. "We're checking, but anybody with loose change can buy a gun in Venice. Look, Captain Barker says you are the best in your business. So why can't we get back to reality—simple murder for money? Underhill owes his publisher a mint. A hundred thousand in one easy grab—wouldn't that be hard for a type like Underhill to resist?"

"And for terrorists, too." Dave rose. "But they resisted, didn't they?" He gave Leppard a tight smile. "Which suggests that you're right about one thing—money is back of it. But a whole hell of a lot more than a hundred thousand dollars." He moved to the door. "Simple, Sergeant? I guess not." He pulled open the door and noise from the detectives' room hit him, laughter, arguments, typewriters, telephones. "Thanks for your time." He let the door fall shut behind him.

The place stood on a narrow street two blocks from the beach in Santa Monica, varnished planks and plate glass glaring in the sun. Angled roofs, skylights, plank-walled outside staircases. The only doors at street level were for cars. Dave locked the Jaguar at the curb, fed a parking meter, dodged a bare-chested boy in shorts and hightop shoes weaving down the sidewalk on a skateboard and wearing bright yellow headphones.

Dave climbed stairs and looked in at an open second-story door. Women in smocks worked at long tables inside. The room was wide as the building. Machines showed glints of metal under fluorescent lights. The women worked the machines by hand. He couldn't make out what material they were die-cutting, embossing, and stapling. It shone like metal in reds, greens, blues, gold. No one noticed him, so he stepped inside.

When his eyes adjusted from the day-glare, he saw Sarah Winger on a high stool at a drafting table, pushing around T-squares, triangles, pencils. He went to her, edging between the women, young, middle-aged, old, assembling slices of coated paper into festive shapes. Only one or two gave him a glance. A fat girl in short-shorts bustled past with a red plastic basket of finished work. She bumped him with a wide hip, and didn't apologize, or seem to hear his apology or want it. She looked as if there simply wasn't time. Everybody here looked as if there wasn't time.

"Christmas tree ornaments?" he said to Sarah Winger.

She looked up, surprised. A green plastic triangle slid down the tilt of the drafting table. She caught it. "Do I know you?" She peered up between false eyelashes from under very blue eye shadow, which intensified the blue of her eyes. "No, I don't. But I saw you yesterday. At the marina. The brown Jaguar. Who are you? What do you want? I'm very busy."

"It's only July," Dave said.

"February wouldn't be too early," she said. "I'm getting calls from buyers right now, wondering where their shipments are. You can't believe the nervousness of people."

Some of the ornaments dangled on strings from rafters. Dave studied them. "Handsome," he said. "You design them all yourself?"

"Santa's helpers aren't what they used to be," she said. She touched the sharp tip of a blue pencil to her lips and bent over her very crisp drawings on a glaring white board. "You don't run a boutique," she said, and carefully drew a serpentine, using a French curve made of amber plastic. "And you certainly don't buy for a department store. There isn't a department store article on you." She gave him a quick, raffish glance. "Unless it's your underwear."

"I forget," he said. "Tell me about the Gernsbachs. Where have they gone? I have to find them."

She stopped drawing and frowned at him. "Are you a police officer? Is it about Adam Streeter? Their neighbor?"

"No," Dave said, "and yes. You want to answer my question?"

"If you're not a police officer, you have no right to ask."

He showed her his license and told her a lie. "I'm investigating for his life insurance company. It's routine."

"Where it might have been suicide?" She went back to work.

"That's right. The Gernsbachs. Special friends of yours?"

"Lily, yes. We went to art school together. She had a lovely talent, a real talent. I didn't—which is why I design and manufacture expensive Christmas tree ornaments. I wanted to paint. So did she, till she met Harry Gernsbach. What a waste. I mean, I'm sorry for his childhood in a concentration camp—but he hasn't an artistic bone in his body."

"Where have they gone?" Dave said. "She left you her key, and said to feed her cat. She didn't tell you then where they were going, how long they'd be gone?"

She sat back and studied her handiwork. "Like it?"

"It looks like an Eskimo ivory carving, a walrus tusk. What do they call it? Scrimshaw work, right?"

"Right." She cocked an eyebrow. "You are a man of discernment. Lily didn't say where they were going. She was in and out of here—not here, but my apartment upstairs—in twenty seconds flat. It wasn't like her. She hated to hurry."

"Was she frightened?" Dave said.

"Frightened?" Sarah Winger frowned. "Of what? Why?"

"The Gernsbachs' apartment has French doors that face those of Adam and Chrissie Streeter."

"That poor child," Sarah Winger said. "What's going to become of her now?"

"She has a mother," Dave said. "Of sorts."

"Yes, I've heard about her," Sarah Winger said. "She does not sound like the answer. Chrissie and Adam got along so well." A shadow crossed the thick makeup of the determinedly youthful middle-aged face. "But it wasn't meant to last, was it? I mean—he was a man who lived dangerously." She tilted her head, forehead wrinkled. "They're saying on the news that someone murdered him. That Mike Underhill who worked for him. Is that the truth?"

"If I thought so," Dave said, "I wouldn't be here."

"It could have been that clergyman," Sarah Winger said. "They had a terrible argument." She blinked the long false lashes at the rafters. "When, last week sometime. I was sitting with Lily in her bedroom. Adam Streeter's study was straight across from there. And we couldn't help overhear—the priest was shouting so. He was absolutely furious. They literally fought, struggled, wrestled, I mean. That we could see—but the sunlight was so bright on the patio we didn't know really what happened, which man was which. Then it was over as suddenly as it had started."

"Chrissie didn't mention this to me," Dave said.

"She must have been out. With Dan'l Chapman. At the beach, the pier, sailing, maybe. He's good to her. Adam's too busy to take her usually. Dan'l is always ready for whatever she wants. Poor child, I think he's in love with her."

"He is," Dave said. "You can't identify the priest?"

The fat girl came to the drawing table, panting, her bangs damp with sweat. "We're getting awful low on staples, Miz Winger. I don't think there's enough to last the day out."

Miz Winger told Dave, "I never saw him before and I couldn't see him all that well. Smallish, I'd say. Glasses. Partly bald." She told the fat girl, "Then take the truck and run over to Pitzer's and get what we need. Tell Ralph to phone me for confirmation." She dropped keys into the fat girl's hand, who waddled away, looking efficient.

"Lily Gernsbach didn't say they were going to Washington?"

"D.C.?" Sarah Winger's eyebrows rose. "Oh, you mean for the Senate hearings on the collapsing savings and loan industry. My God, what a dreary man that Harry Gernsbach is. Awful accent and all. No, I'm sure she didn't."

"Who was going to pick up their car from the airport?"

"Perhaps someone at Harry's office." Sarah Winger took up a handful of colored pencils and began shading in the sharp outlines on the bristol board. "Lily didn't ask me. Only to feed Trinket. What a name for that savage brute." She worked in silence for a moment. The machines clanked. The shiny paper whispered. She said to her deftly moving hands, "Maybe they didn't fly. They own a beautiful big boat."

"Then why leave the cat behind?" Dave said.

"Because she's not like other cats," Sarah Winger said. "She has no fear of the water. She tries to swim to shore. And the Coast Guard has issued notice. Twice was enough. They will not come on the double to rescue Trinket again."

"What was the priest furious about?" Dave said.

"His son was killed," she said, "and he blamed Adam."

The woman was a fresh-faced forty. She looked at him with frightened eyes through a screen door of bright new aluminum that contrasted with the weathered shingle siding of the house. The house crouched under gloomy deodars behind a shingle-sided church. The house was one-storied, typical of Sierra Madre, a town that had changed some since he had known it in his boyhood—but not on these backstreets. He had visited this very church, St. Matthias, as a chorister. He had owned a clear, sweet soprano voice in those days and, in a red cassock and starchy white lace-trimmed cotta, with his blond hair, he'd looked angelic. He had not been angelic, but that was another story.

Now he said to the woman, whose hair was cut sensibly short, who wore blue jeans, a cambric shirt, and jogging shoes without socks, and who wiped anxious, thin fingers on a kitchen towel:

"Reverend Pierce Glendenning, please?" The man's name was lettered Gothic style in flaking gold on a cracked black signboard posted in ground ivy in front of the church. This was the place. "Is he here?"

"Are you a reporter?" She took hold of the wooden house door to swing it shut. "I'm sorry. We don't want to talk anymore about Rue's death. Not to news people. Please, go away and leave us alone."

"I'm not a reporter." He told her who he was, speaking loudly so as to be heard by whoever lurked back there in the dusky rooms behind her. He held out the ostrich-hide folder with his license for her to read through the screen if she could. "I'm looking into the death of Adam Streeter."

"No." Her eyes opened wide for a second. Since she wore no makeup, it was easy to see her flush. "We didn't know him."

"Mr. Glendenning knew him." Dave tucked away the folder in an inside jacket pocket. "Perhaps he never told you."

A door slammed at the rear of the house. So loudly that it made the young woman jump. Dave left the cool porch with its earth-smelling pots of nasturtiums, geraniums, marigolds set along the wide redwood railing. He went quickly to the corner of the house. Out back, footsteps hammered stairs. Dave ran up the cracked cement driveway alongside the house. In the rear, wooden stairs climbed a steep hill densely overgrown with scruffy shrubs and eucalyptus trees. He caught glimpses of the man, legs for a moment, taking the steps two at a time, a hand hauling him upward by a two-by-four railing, a flash of bare scalp, a glint of spectacles where sunlight found its way down through the thick leafage. The woman came out the back door of the house.

"Leave him alone," she cried. "He had nothing to do with Adam Streeter's death."

Dave glanced at her, then studied again that long zigzag of rickety stairs. He was still bruised, his muscles still ached from jumping that fool fence at Hunsinger's. He smoked too much: he didn't have the wind to get halfway to the top without a rest. He kept telling himself to retire. When was he going to listen? Far above, Glendenning's shoes stopped knocking wood. He had reached a street up there. Dave turned to the woman.

"He shouldn't have run," he said. "It looks like an admission of guilt."

"It isn't," she said sharply. "He didn't kill Adam Streeter. What makes you think he did? How did you find us?"

"He had a violent argument with Streeter," Dave said, "a few days ago. There was a witness. There were two."

"Oh, God," she said miserably. "I begged him not to go." She put fingertips to her mouth like a nerve-shattered ten-year-old, and snatched them away again as if her mother had called to her through the kitchen window not to bite her nails. She said to Dave, "He was grieving, don't you understand? Beside himself with grief. For Rue. Our son. A beautiful, gifted boy. Murdered at twenty-two." Tears brimmed her eyes. Her voice trembled. "Pierce Glendenning is a gentle, kind, caring man. Patient. Understanding."

"And angry," Dave said.

"He couldn't kill anyone," she said.

"Then he won't mind talking to me." Dave held out a card. "Give him this. As soon as he comes back, please. Tell him to call me. If he doesn't call me, I'll go to the police tomorrow morning. Is that clear?"

She nodded numbly, took the card, pushed it into a shirt pocket. Her lips moved, but she decided not to say any more. She turned forlornly and went back inside. The screen door here was old, wood-framed, the mesh black and bulging. He couldn't see through it, but he heard her fingers rattle a hook, and click it closed.

## 7

IT WAS EARLY at Max Romano's. A few afternoon drinkers hung on in the small dark, wood and leather bar. Now and then, laughter came from there, the jingle of ice in glasses. But the dining room was empty except for Dave and Cecil at their usual table in a far corner. The other tables waited under heavy white cloths, candlelight glinting on silver and glass. Good smells of herbs, cheese, garlic drifted in from the kitchen. In front of Cecil, on an oval platter of crushed ice, lay a row of handsome big shrimp.

He hummed over them happily, and rubbed his palms together. "Look at that," he crooned, "will you just look at those beauties."

"I have my oysters," Dave said. "I am content."

"I will not look at oysters." Cecil picked up a shrimp, bit it in two. "Oysters," he said as he chewed, "are alive. You are about to devour a living creature."

Dave's platter of crushed ice held a dozen oysters on the half shell. He squeezed lemon juice over them, lifted one of the shells, rough to the fingers, cold, tilted its contents into his mouth, swallowed it. It was his turn to hum. He grinned at Cecil, who was pulling a disgusted face, and said, "You don't know what's good."

"Shrimp," Cecil said, and finished off the first one. He wiped his fingers on a heavy white napkin. "They are not going to admit it."

"Jimmie Caesar and Dot Yamada," Dave said.

"Those two." Cecil nodded and took a swallow of champagne. "When I told them what I saw and heard, they turned green. Adam Streeter, in their office, at two in the morning? Was I crazy? What was I trying to do to them?"

Dave slid another oyster down his throat. "They hadn't seen you out there, eavesdropping in the hallway?"

Cecil bit another big shrimp in half. "No way." He shook his head. "No light in that hall, except way down at the end. They thought I was toiling away in my sweaty little editing room, didn't they?"

Dave tried the champagne. It lacked edge. It was too far over on the fruity side. The bottle leaned in an ice bucket on the thickly carpeted floor beside his chair. He bent for it, lifted it dripping, squinted at the label. Blurry. He fumbled reading glasses out of his jacket, got them onto his nose, read the vineyard name and the year, and twisted the bottle back into the ice. The year was all that was wrong. He wouldn't order 1973 again. Not with that label. He put the glasses away, and finished off three more oysters. "It is one of the advantages," Cecil said, "of being black. One of the unnumbered advantages."

*"Invisible man,"* Dave said.

Cecil nodded, working on another shrimp. "Only how Mr. Ellison saw it—it was a disadvantage. Mostly."

"They're afraid of being drawn into a murder case," Dave said. "Afraid of what their infantile trick led to. And I can't say I blame them."

"Looked at each other with their mouths hanging open," Cecil said, "and looked at me, like their heads were on one swivel, and both of them started talking at once."

"You imagined it?" Dave said. "It never happened?"

"I must have it in for them," Cecil said. "Why else would I make up a story like that? I'm trying to lose them their jobs. They're in the way of my unbounded ambition, right? Another pushy nigger."

"They didn't say that," Dave said.

"They didn't have to. Not to me. But they'll say it to somebody, if I make it known, won't they? And you know how that will go. There are two of them and only one of me. Odd man out, right?"

"Don't make it known," Dave said. "It doesn't go anywhere."

The shrimp were gone. Cecil looked forlornly at the heap of coral-crisp shells on the platter of ice. Dave's oysters were gone, too. A waiter named Avram, a stocky youngster whose large soft brown eyes always yearned at Cecil, came in his gold velveteen jacket and took the platters away. Cecil wiped his mouth and fingers on the napkin again.

"What *does* go somewhere?" he asked.

"Possibly the father of young Glendenning," Dave said.

Cecil's eyebrows went up. "The reporter killed in Los Inocentes?"

"Afterward, the father went to Streeter. He's an Anglican priest. They had a loud argument. They had a fight."

Cecil started to ask about this when Max Romano came with a smile, bearing plates that steamed—lamb kidneys for Dave, tournedos of beef for Cecil. Dave was very likely Max's oldest customer—he'd come to the place first in 1947, '48. On the west side then, Max had moved it to a site half a block below Hollywood Boulevard, but street crime had scared off customers there, and now he was back on the west side. This place was not quite the same as the old one, but it would come nearer when the stained glass went in. It was being fashioned now in the workshop of some artisan who took his sweet time. Dave looked up at the smiling Max. In the old days he'd had thick curly black hair, well oiled, and teeth that made his grin legendary. Only thin strands of hair remained, carefully combed across his scalp. And gold patches glinted in his teeth. But a more important change showed itself tonight— Max was losing weight. He had always been a fat man, comfortable in his fatness. Tonight his clothes hung loosely on him. It struck Dave abruptly that Max was old—well past seventy. He said with real anxiety:

"How are you, Max? Are you all right?"

Max set the plates down, and gave Dave a gentle smile. "You're worried, my friend?" He tugged at the spare cloth of his jacket. "You think I'm wasting away, eh? It is a diet—imagine me on a diet." He chuckled. "It's high blood pressure, Dave. The doctors say I have to lose seventy-five pounds. I eat a carrot stick, a stalk of celery, a piece of fish"—he made a circle with his fingers, diamond rings winking in the candlelight—"this big. They want me to live forever." The corners of his mouth turned down. "Do you call that living?"

"I want you to live forever, too," Dave said.

Max touched his shoulder. "Bless you, my friend. I am going to try"—he sighed and wagged his head dolefully—"but it is torture." He looked for a moment at their plates and turned sharply away. "Enjoy your dinner," he said weakly, and hurried off to meet a quartet of customers pushing in at the door, laughing and chattering. Dave looked after him.

"He's all right," Cecil said to Dave. "He's fine."

"I hope so." Dave wondered where the gloom came from, and leaned for the champagne bottle again, and filled their glasses. Cecil smiled at him as he did so, and Dave mustered a smile in return. That was better. Cecil was the present. And the future. They were all that mattered. He said, "There are also the Gernsbachs. Why did they run away? Where did they go? What did they see that scared them?"

"A man in a preacher's collar," Cecil said, "shooting their neighbor in the head. Sounds scary enough to me."

"I have to find them." Dave picked up his fork. "You want to help me? Are you free tonight?"

"Aw, you broke the magic spell." Cecil pushed back a shirt cuff. On his bony wrist was a large black watch, spiny with stops. He read it, and his eyes opened wide. "I am due back in the newsroom in exactly twenty-eight minutes." He looked panicked, stuffed his mouth, burned himself, hastily gulped champagne. "Shit. What happened to all the time?"

"I keep asking myself that," Dave said.

The night guard in the cedar and glass gatehouse was a stout, gray-haired woman. She looked soldierly, with the square jutting jaw of a drill sergeant. But the magazine open on the little shelf beside her was *Woman's Day,* and a straw carryall in a corner behind her showed knitting needles and skeins of yarn in rose and lavender. Dave braked the Jaguar, rolled down the window, said to her:

"Dan'l Chapman, please. My name is Brandstetter."

She studied him with gray, grandmotherly eyes. Sternly. Was she going to ask whether he had washed behind his ears? "Are you expected?" she said.

"He won't be surprised," Dave said.

She took down the phone. "I will," she said, and told the phone, "Dan'l—there's a Mr. Braniff or something here." Dave sighed, opened the car door, got out. "Says he wants to see you." Dave slid the folder out of his inside jacket pocket, let it fall open, held it through the gatehouse door for her to read. She squinted, pushed her head out, nearsighted. "Private investigator," she said. "I think you should come down to the gate, please." She hung the phone back on its wall bracket. "He'll be here in a minute."

"You take your responsibilities seriously," Dave said.

"I'm paid to do that." Half-moon reading glasses lay on the shelf. She put them on, blinked at the magazine for a moment, looked at Dave over the glasses. "He's a juvenile, and he's at home alone."

"I see." Dave put his folder away. "Did Mike Underhill come to see Adam Streeter the night he was killed?"

"Police already asked me that," she said. "Answer's no."

"Did they ask you if you saw him leave about three A.M.?"

"No"—she flipped a page of the magazine and bent her head over it again—"but the answer to that is no, too."

Dave gazed through the wire mesh of the gates at the soft ground lighting among the big azaleas lining the clean-swept blacktop of the drive. "I sometimes have to stay up all night in my line of work. It isn't easy not to fall asleep." He turned back to her. "Do you ever fall asleep?"

"When you have to stay up every night"—she still mused over the magazine, color photos of sandwiches frilly with lettuce—"keeping awake gets to be a habit. Nothing to it after a while."

"Then you saw Harry Gernsbach leave," Dave said, "about three thirty, four?"

She took off the glasses and stared at him. "I did not. Why would he do that? He keeps regular hours. Very regular. Set your watch by Harry Gernsbach leaving and coming home."

"What about a clergyman, a priest?" Dave said. "Name of Pierce Glendenning. Did he come that night? To see Adam Streeter, I mean?"

"Police didn't ask me that, either," she said. "But you need batting practice." She almost smiled. "You just struck out." She turned her head. "Here comes Dan'l."

The air pushing in off the dark water was chilly, and the boy came in a sweater, a windbreaker, hands thrust into the pockets of corduroy pants. These made him look less scrawny than had the trunks and cutoff shirt of yesterday, less of a child. The wind ruffled his red hair. He pushed it out of his eyes and squinted through the gates at Dave.

"Dan'l," the guard said, "do you know this man?"

"You got his name wrong," Dan'l said. "It's Brandstetter. Dave. Yes, I know him, Clara. It's okay, honest." His smile at the woman in her square starchy tan uniform, gun on her hip, was fleeting. His eyes were worried. He asked Dave, "Is it about Chrissie? Is something wrong?"

"Nothing we don't both know about." Dave got behind the wheel of the Jaguar again. But the gates didn't open. He looked at Clara, who looked at Dan'l, her mouth a thin line.

"I wish your parents were home," she said.

"Come on, Clara." Dan'l clutched the wire mesh like a kitten in a pound. "I'm not six years old anymore."

"Six, sixteen," she snorted, "what's the difference?" But she opened the gates.

Dave parked the Jaguar in shadow inside the grounds and far from the gates. Dan'l started to get out. Dave said, "Just a second. I have some questions, first. The Gernsbachs' boat—is it moored near here?"

"Sure," Dan'l said. "Only not now. It's not there, now."

"I didn't think so. Okay—did you ever hear Adam or Chrissie mention Rue Glendenning's father? A priest?"

"Glendenning? The kid from UCLA who came to ask Adam how to be a foreign correspondent?" Dan'l's face was no more than a pale shadow, but Dave saw puzzlement in it. "No. Where does his father figure?"

"You made a play on words," Dave said.

"Ho-ho," Dan'l said. "They never mentioned him to me."

"Right—question three." Dave opened his door and got out. Dan'l got out on the other side. "Close it quietly." Some windows were alight in the condominiums, second-and third-floor windows. Dan'l clicked his door shut. Dave did the same, and went to the boy. He said softly, "If I gave you ropes and so on, could you climb to the roofs up there, cross them, and drop down onto the balcony of Streeter's workroom?"

"Who needs ropes?" Leaf-mottled ground light played on Dan'l's eager face. "It should be easy. Come on." He moved off, soundless in Nikes. "I'll show you."

Dave followed him in and out of shadow, past the silent fronts of the jogged buildings. As they moved on, the air grew cooler. The fence held access gates, locked—tenants who owned boats would have keys. The boats rocked asleep at their moorings beyond the fence, under stretched blue canvas coverings, water lapping softly at their sleek white hulls, masts tilting at the sky like pointers in the hands of so many teachers at one vast blackboard.

They reached the far end of the buildings. Trash modules, blue metal with sloping lids, stood here against garage walls. Dan'l swung up on one of these, stood, grabbed rafter ends, hiked himself to a garage roof, scrambled to his feet, and stood grinning down at Dave. "See?" Dave saw. Beyond the boy lay another easy pull-up to a second-story roof. From there, one more light-bodied lift would put him on the highest roofs.

"Good," Dave said. "Go quietly, right? I'll meet you there."

Even in darkness, the lock on number twenty-seven was easy to pick. He closed the door softly behind him. Light came through the French doors into the big drowsing Chinese room from the pool patio. He walked quickly to the spiral staircase, where he slipped off his shoes. Even in stocking feet, his steps brought soft resonance from the dark metal. At the top, he put the shoes on. A light switch was on the wall just inside the workroom door. He lifted it with the edge of a hand. The desk lamp flickered on. He pressed the switch that controlled the drapes, and they swished back. He unlocked and opened the French doors. The flowerpots still lay there, the earth that had spilled from them dry now, the stalks and leaves of the plants withered.

He sat at the desk, facing the keyboard of the computer, the computer's empty gray face. Frowning, he let his gaze rove—and there lay the thick black book. He remembered Chrissie standing here, her thumb nervously rubbing the corners of its pages. He pulled the book to him and opened it at the last of those scraps of paper Streeter had laid in it to mark references he wanted to get back to and never would. He had highlighted a name in yellow with a broad marking pen—*Lothrop Zorn, Colonel, U.S. Marine Corps, retired.* Dave heard a soft sound behind him, half turned, and something cold poked his left temple. Not a gun barrel—a finger.

"Bang, you're dead," Dan'l Chapman said.

"As easy as that," Dave said. He looked down the room at the balcony. "Any trouble with the flowerpots?"

"Not me." Dan'l, panting a little, but pleased with himself, perched on the Turkish inlaid cabinet. "I didn't knock those over." He laughed. "Pretty neat, right? I always wanted to do that. What I needed was authorization, right? Being a kid is a hard thing to get over, having to ask permission."

"You'll manage," Dave said. "Could Underhill have done it?"

Dan'l blinked, scratched his acne, frowned. "Could he? I don't know. He wasn't fat or old or anything. I guess so, probably. You think he killed Adam?"

"The police think so. For that hundred thousand Streeter got from the TV producer."

"Jesus," Dan'l whispered to himself. "What a shit."

"How could he get past Clara without her seeing him?"

"He couldn't. But there's a cut in the fence. I noticed it two or three days ago. Along the back there, farther than where we went. It's cut and bent back. Was. My dad reported it when I showed it to him. They've mended it now."

"Meaning he could have come in from the water, arrived in a boat, cut the fence, and then climbed here as you did." Dave closed the book, stood up. "Shut the windows and the curtains, all right? We'd better get out of here." He picked up the book, thinking of how fast Glendenning ran up that long flight of stairs. It could have been simple fright that drove him. Or he could have been in excellent shape. Everybody jogged these days, everybody played tennis or racquet ball. Even preachers, he supposed. Why not? Dan'l came back down the room and raised his eyebrows at the book.

"You taking that?" he said.

"I'll return it." Dave moved toward the door with Dan'l following. "There may be a lead in it. Streeter was using it in his work." Dave switched off the workroom light. They moved along the shadowy gallery toward the stairs.

Dan'l said, "Why don't you think Underhill did it?"

"Because someone went to a lot of trouble to frame him." Dave stood on one foot, then the other, to slip off his shoes.

Book and shoes held in one hand, he took hold of the cold steel stair rail and started down. "Men in camouflage combat outfits—ever seen any of them hanging around this neighborhood?"

"You're kidding," Dan'l said. "You mean shooting a film, or something like that?"

"I don't know what I mean," Dave said. "I wish I did."

## 8

NAKED BESIDE DAVE in the wide dark bed on the sleeping loft of the rear building, Cecil sighed and stirred long arms and legs. Dave opened his eyes. Stars showed through the skylight overhead. He peered at the red numbers of the bedside clock. Four ten. Cecil had turned his back. Dave shifted position to lie against his back and to drape an arm gently over his lanky form. Cecil murmured, laughed softly, and moved Dave's hand downward. Then he gave a sudden jerk, and sat up. Teeth and eye whites showed in the darkness.

"Somebody's out in the courtyard. Listen." Footsteps crackled the dry leaves fallen from the old oak out there onto the bricks. Dave rolled aside, sat up, swung his feet to the floor, and reached for his clothes. That the bed moved told him Cecil was doing the same on his side. And more quickly. His tall, lean shape was at the chest of drawers, rattling it open, hands rummaging among clothes. He came up with Dave's SIG Sauer automatic, a tool he hated and feared. Its metal glinted in the starlight. He started toward the stairs.

"Stay here with that," Dave told him, "and cover me."

He zipped up his jeans, tucked in a T-shirt. Barefoot, he passed Cecil and went down the plank stairs, cool to his soles, thumping under his heels. He wasn't awake yet. In his dream, those night commandos of Hunsinger's had moored a motor gig in the black waters behind the condominiums and clambered out. Bright blades had clipped the hurricane fencing, strong hands in black gloves had parted the cut place. The men had ducked under it, guns in their hands, and like skinny young Dan'l earlier this night, begun to clamber up the buildings ghostly in their ground lights. The dream had left a cold place in his belly. His heart thudded as he reached the foot of the stairs and began to move toward the front door. Why didn't he turn on lamps? No one had threatened him. He didn't turn on lamps. He wished there were a window in the wall with the door. He wished the door were not solid. His hand moved to turn the deadbolt, unhitch the chain, but he didn't do these things. He stood motionless and strained to hear. The footsteps crunching leaves drew nearer. A hand fumbled the heavy black iron knocker. It banged. The sound ricocheted down the long wooden room.

"Who is it?" Dave called, and stepped aside.

No one answered. Dave put his back against the wall next to the door. He looked up at the loft. Cecil had put on white jeans. These were all Dave could see of him, standing at the top of the stairs—these and the glint of the gun he held straight out, pointed at the door. A throat was cleared outside in the night.

"Is that Mr. Brandstetter?" The voice sounded afraid.

"The name is on the mailbox," Dave said. "Who's asking?"

The throat was cleared again. "Pierce Glendenning."

Dave unbolted and unchained the door and pulled it open. Glendenning was in nonclerical clothes, a tweed jacket, polo shirt with broad green stripes, chinos, and old hightop calfskin shoes. He looked young, the square, not-quite-handsome face smooth, as if life had rarely troubled him much. It was the thinning gray hair that aged him, and the unstylish wire-rim glasses. And the panic that swam in the pale hazel eyes behind those glasses now. "Come in," Dave told him.

"I didn't kill Adam Streeter," Glendenning said. He stepped past Dave, and Dave caught the smell of sweat—not from physical exertion, from fear. Dave closed the door and touched a light switch beside it. Lamps went on at either end of the long, comfortable corduroy couch that faced the big fireplace halfway down the room. Glendenning said, "I wanted to kill him, but I didn't do it." Then he caught sight of Cecil standing on the loft, still pointing the gun. "Dear God," he said.

Dave smiled faintly at Cecil. "You can put it away now."

Cecil relaxed his stiff-armed pose. "That's nice," he said, and moved out of sight. Dave heard the drawer of the chest open, close. When Cecil came loose-jointedly down the stairs, he was pulling a T-shirt over his head. He smiled at Glendenning, who looked frightened of him, while Dave introduced them. "Don't take the gun personally," Cecil said, shaking his hand. "We didn't know who you might be. Friends don't often come calling at this time of day."

"I'm sorry." Glendenning's face reddened. "I forgot the hour. I . . . it took me . . . I had to work up my resolve."

Dave moved off toward the couch. "Come sit down."

"I don't want to keep you," Glendenning said. "It's the wrong time. I've interrupted your sleep."

"What about coffee?" Cecil said.

Standing back to the fireplace, Dave said, "There's a lot to talk about. You're in deep trouble, Reverend."

Glendenning looked sick. "I didn't know anyone saw me."

"And heard you," Dave said. "A close neighbor of Streeter's, just across the patio—Lily Gernsbach. And a visiting friend, Sarah Winger."

Did Glendenning hear? He looked stunned. At last, he said faintly to Cecil, "Yes, coffee, thank you," and nodded. He turned Dave a look of weary surrender and walked toward the couch.

Dave asked Cecil, "Shall I fix the coffee?"

"You talk," Cecil said. "I'll fix it."

"I must have been literally blind with rage." Glendenning dropped numbly onto the couch. He sat forward, elbows on knees, hands clasped, fingers knitted, head bowed. He might have been praying, only he seemed not up to it. "You read those expressions and you think you know what they mean, but you don't." He looked up wanly. "Not until it happens to you."

Cecil went out and left the door to the courtyard open. The cool air that comes an hour before sunrise washed into the room. The canyon was still quiet. No cars passed along the main road below. The crickets had left off. So had the mockingbirds, those all-night singers. Distantly Dave heard the door of the cookshack open, heard Cecil work the hand pump for spring water and rattle the filled teakettle onto a burner of the mighty stove.

"Streeter's windows were open," Dave said to Glendenning. "And directly opposite, the windows of Gernsbach's master bedroom were also open."

"I went to kill him that day," Glendenning said.

Dave sat on the raised stone hearth. "With what?"

"I'd written him a letter. I wish I had that letter back."

"His papers were stolen by whoever killed him," Dave said. "The police don't have them."

"They'll get them," Glendenning said cheerlessly. "And they'll read my letter and know I threatened to kill him. He phoned and asked me to come see him so he could explain." Glendenning's laugh was brief and bitter. "As if he could explain away the wanton killing of an innocent young boy."

"Streeter didn't kill him. Wantonly or otherwise."

Glendenning sat up, stiff with indignation. "He gave him wanton advice. Reckless, heedless, irresponsible. Rue trusted him. And he sent him off to be killed."

"So you wrote the letter," Dave said, "and Streeter asked you to come see him, and you went to kill him to avenge your son's death—a life for a life. How were you going to do that? How were you going to kill him? With what?"

"My son's gun. He'd bought it after Streeter advised him to go to Central America. If he wanted to get off to a running start as a foreign correspondent. To go where—"

"Where the action was," Dave said.

"Rue was a gentle, quiet boy," Glendenning said. "I don't mean he wasn't manly, but he didn't believe in violence. If it hadn't been for Adam Streeter, he'd never have dreamed of buying a firearm, something that could kill another human being."

"Gentle, quiet, but ambitious, right?" Dave said. "In a hurry to make his mark in the world."

A corner of Glendenning's mouth twisted sadly. "I didn't say he wasn't young, did I? Aren't we always in a hurry to leave childhood behind, get out on our own, prove ourselves strong and capable?"

"It was a Desert Eagle pistol, wasn't it?" Dave said. "And that was what you fought over, there in Streeter's workroom. And that was why the fight ended so abruptly. Because he was bigger and stronger and got it away from you."

Glendenning bent forward again, hung his head again. "Yes," he murmured. "It was easy for him. He laughed at me as if I were a little boy, opened a drawer, dropped the gun inside."

"Where it stayed," Dave said, "until he tried to defend himself with it against attackers stronger than he was, who took it away from him and killed him with it. Was it your son who had it fitted with a silencer?"

Glendenning shook his head. "I did that. Later."

"Why did your son leave the gun behind?"

"The airline wouldn't let him take it."

"Right. And Streeter knew that. So buying the gun was your son's own idea. Which suggests to me that Streeter gave him a fair picture of the danger he was flying into. I don't call that irresponsible."

Glendenning started to answer, and Cecil came in with mugs of coffee on a tray. He set the tray on the hearth near Dave. Spoons lay on the tray beside a squat brown pottery pitcher of cream, a squat brown sugar bowl. Glendenning wanted his coffee black; Dave wanted a cigarette with his coffee and climbed to the loft to get the pack and his lighter. He heard Cecil stir sugar and cream into his coffee and ask:

"Did your son talk to you about Los Inocentes—what he hoped to find there?"

"He wanted to get to the insurgents, the rebels, to live with them if he could, to tell their side of the story." Glendenning gave a brief dismal laugh. "And they killed him, didn't they?"

"That's how the government tells it," Cecil said.

Dave found his cigarettes and lighter on the bedside stand and came down out of the loft darkness into the lamplight again. He sat down on the hearth, lit a cigarette, tried his coffee, and thought of lacing it with brandy. He looked down the room to the bar in deep shadow under the new section of loft. But he didn't go there.

Glendenning said, "He also hoped to prove there were American special forces fighting the rebels in the hills. Something Washington always denies."

"If it's true," Cecil said, "maybe they killed him."

Glendenning brooded over his coffee mug. "I'm sick about the whole thing. Sick to the heart."

"When you leave here," Dave said, "go to Parker Center and find Detective Sergeant Jeff Leppard and tell him where the Desert Eagle came from."

Glendenning's head jerked up. His glasses magnified the dismay in his eyes. "Must I? What good will it do?"

"They're trying to hang the killing on Mike Underhill," Dave said. "A man who worked for him. And I don't think it was Underhill. You can't let them convict the wrong man."

"Why was he the wrong man? Anyone could have used the gun. I didn't have it that night. Adam Streeter had it." Glendenning got up quickly, set the mug on the hearth, stood talking down at them. "What you're asking me to do is bring disgrace not just on myself, but on my wife, my parish, my whole denomination. I'm morally guilty, I know that. Guilty before God, and don't think I'm not miserable about it. But I did not kill that man."

"It was your son's gun," Dave said, "fitted with your silencer. You were serious enough about killing him to buy that. You hated him, and I wonder if that stopped. I wonder if, a few days later, you didn't buy a pair of wire cutters."

Glendenning gaped. "What are you talking about?"

"The guard on the gate at Streeter's place says you didn't pass her that night. But that night someone cut the fence in back of the place. Someone crossed the marina by water in the dark, cut the fence, and—"

"No. Absolutely not. Fantastic."

"My guess could have been wrong. That Streeter took the gun away from you and kept it."

"He did. But even if he hadn't—I wasn't at the marina that night. I was at County USC Medical Center. A parishioner was taken violently sick—Tom Fraser. Fine man. My deacon. I was there with his family, wife, daughter, son, until the emergency surgery was completed, and they told us he was out of danger. I got the call around midnight, and it was daylight by the time I left the hospital."

"And the doctor's name?" Dave said.

"Scheinwald," Glendenning said. "Ask him, if you must."

"If there isn't any need," Dave said, "then you can tell Leppard about the gun, can't you? And save yourself embarrassment later. Because eventually he'll come asking you about it. And if he doesn't, Underhill's lawyers are bound to."

"I'll lie. I'll say it was stolen. Why not?" Glendenning smiled wretchedly. "I'm damned anyway."

"You're too hard on yourself," Dave said.

"Oh, no." Glendenning's laugh was sharp and despairing. "I meant to kill that man. And I would have done it, too, if he hadn't been quicker than I was." He turned away, shoulders slumping. His voice was hollow. "I lost my son.

And then I lost my soul." He moved heavy-footed out of the lamplight. "I'm no longer fit to be a priest." He stepped out the open door into the courtyard. "What in the world am I going to do with the rest of my life?" The crackle of dry leaves under his shoes grew faint and passed out of hearing. Distantly, a car door slammed, an engine started, the noise of the car faded out down the canyon. Dave switched off the lamps. Gray light filled the doorway.

"It's morning," Cecil said.

"Not for him," Dave said.

"County USC Medical is near my workplace," Cecil said. "You want me to check out Dr. Scheinwald before I take up my oar in the galley? The Tom Fraser family?"

"I'll be forever in your debt," Dave said.

## 9

THE CHAPEL WAS a copy of an English country church. It stood on a rise among trees. Trees shadowed a lawn that sloped down to a curve of roadway where cars waited, limousines, taxis. The funeral service was over. The coffin had been lowered to the crematorium under the chapel. An electronic organ run by a computer played on to the empty pews, the damp-smelling flowers. And those who had come to say goodbye to Adam Streeter straggled off through the long shadows of the trees. Bronze grave markers were embedded in the grass. Now and then, someone turned an ankle on one of these, or snagged a toe or heel on one, and stumbled a little, to be caught and steadied by another mourner. Car doors slammed. Engines started.

Dave stood next to a lawyer called Albright in the porch of the chapel and watched the crowd leave. *He had friends all over the world.* Chrissie had been right about that. The skin tones had varied from intense African blue-black to the whitest Scandinavian, the body types and sizes from miniature Thais to titanic Germans. Turbans and spectacular caps had covered heads. Saris and caftans in wild colors fluttered now in the late afternoon breeze. Albright, too, must have been thinking about this multinational, multiracial, multireligious character of the crowd. He said:

"Why didn't she come? Everyone else on earth did."

"It looks that way." Dave shrugged. "I guess she's used to keeping out of sight. Streeter didn't want Chrissie to know about her. Or Chrissie's mother. Particularly."

"I know that," Albright said. "But it no longer obtains." He was a trim young man in a summer weight suit and neatly clipped beard. There wasn't any tone to his voice. He had a fine tan and he stood erect, but the voice made him sound worn out, tired to death. "And it sure as hell won't obtain when Brenda Streeter reads the will—the ex-wife."

"She's getting cut out of everything these days," Dave said. "Maybe she won't even notice Fleur's little legacy. I'd gauge she isn't often sober."

"She's always greedy," Albright said in his dead voice. "She'll scratch and claw to get it all, if she can."

Inside the chapel back of them the quavery organ went silent in the middle of a phrase. Fastenings on the carved double doors rattled. A bald man in a dark suit and modest tie swung the doors shut. Steel bars slid into place inside.

"Speak of the devil." Albright jerked his chin. Ivy climbed the chapel walls. And past a leafy corner of the building, Brenda Streeter, in shiny tight black satin, a black pillbox hat with a veil, and keeping a firm grip on Chrissie's arm, led the blind girl away. Chrissie was the taller. The black mohair suit her mother had put her into didn't fit, pulled at the armpits, and Dave bet the waist of the skirt was safety-pinned. She wore dark glasses. Her face was wet from weeping. Brenda's wasn't. She swished Chrissie's slim white cane like a sword to fend off enemies. Dave turned from watching them, and Albright had stepped behind a stone pillar. "Quiet," he said. "I want her to think I've gone." Both men waited until mother and daughter were out of hearing. "Witch," Albright said. "I'm sorry for that poor kid."

Dave knew Brenda's car, a dark red Seville. He had driven her and Chrissie in it to her apartment the other day, Dan'l following in Adam's black, low-slung, knife-edged sports car. A man got out of the Seville now and opened doors, a youngish man with a mane of oily black curls well down over his collar, dark skin, dark glasses, shirt open, gold neck chains glinting on a muscular chest. His biceps bulged. He closed the car doors—Brenda in the front seat, Chrissie in the back—jogged around the front of the car, got into the driver's seat, slammed the door, and rolled the car away. It was three or four years old, but it shone like new. Maybe he rubbed it down with his hair. Dave said, "Who's Mr. Universe?"

"Ken Kastouros." Albright gazed after the car. "Not the chauffeur. The lover. In for the money—right?"

"If Brenda can hang on to Chrissie," Dave said. "Otherwise there won't be any money. Can you stop that? It wasn't what her father wanted—not as I understand it."

"Chrissie doesn't get the principal, not from her grandmother's will or her father's. Not till she's twenty-one. Substantial monthly payments, but not millions. Not yet."

"Chrissie talked about getting married," Dave said.

"That's a common mistake. In some legal respects it would make her a woman, but the state would still control the money while she was underage. That's how it is in California."

"So with Brenda as her guardian," Dave said, "Brenda will be in charge of how such money as does come is spent."

Albright grunted. "It will be spent on Brenda."

"And Ken," Dave said. "You can't prevent that?"

"Brenda won in a walkover—grandma dead, daddy dead, no other living relatives. She's a drunk and takes too many pills, but she's not a criminal. You'll tell Fleur now?"

"It's on my way home," Dave said.

Albright pushed back a snowy cuff to read a gold Rolex. "I have a plane to catch in less than an hour." He nodded at Dave. "Do it. I'll be grateful. I was going to tell her here. If you've got her phone number"—he peered around the cemetery in the sunset light—"I can call her, if I can find a phone"—he looked at the shut-up chapel doors— "anyplace."

"I'll take care of it," Dave said.

The flower shop was a low-roofed, deep-eaved bungalow on a corner lot a few blocks from Sarah Winger's place. But Winger's building was new, and the bungalow dated from World War I. Maybe it wasn't technically a bungalow— it had a single square upstairs room, windows all around. The front yard, picketed with unpainted lath, was a nursery for young plants in wooden flats under redwood beams hung with drooping cheesecloth to temper the sun. The side yard was fenced by six-foot-high planks, but he could see the tops of young trees, Brazilian peppers, Japanese maples, longleaf pines, three kinds of eucalyptus.

He turned onto the side street. The old garage leaned, its roof slumped. On a cracked cement driveway, the new lavender van nosed the garage doors. He pulled in behind it, left the Jaguar there, and pushed a plank gate into a backyard where arbors sheltered more little plants, on the ground, on unpainted wooden tables, on shelves. Ferns and vines trailed from hanging decorator pots. There was a plank workshop and a potting shed walled with lattice. Dave walked along beside the bungalow among the young trees in tubs and breathed the rich dark odor of damp earth.

His shadow fell long and pleated up the porch steps. He climbed the steps. On the porch, racks of bent wire and of doweled wood held new rakes, hoes, cultivators, trowels, cotton gloves, kneeling pads. Coils of green garden hose were stacked beside clear plastic sacks of mulch, paper sacks of fertilizer. Inside a tall oval of glass in the front door hung a CLOSED sign in red letters on white cardboard.

That was funny. His watch told him it was past five. But these racks had wheels under them. Maybe there weren't many thieves equipped to steal potted plants. Even if there were a black market for them, it would involve a lot of work for little return. But this stuff on the porch was easily marketable. There were even two power lawnmowers in shiny red enamel, price tags hanging off their handles.

Shielding his eyes with a hand, he turned and looked down the walk to the front gate. There was no lock on it, and the lath pickets weren't any use at all to keep trespassers out. Fleur would wheel the racks indoors at closing time, the garden hose, the mowers, maybe even heave the fertilizer sacks in there. CLOSED? He peered through the glass. Inside was a counter with a cash register, sheets of green wrapping paper for bouquets, buckets of cut gladiolus, carnations, delphiniums behind tall glass refrigerator doors. More hanging ferns. Vases, jars, bowls. But no human beings. The doorbell looked corroded but he thumbed it. Nothing chimed or buzzed in the house. He rapped the glass.

"Hello. Anybody here?"

No one answered. He tried the latch. Locked. Her van was back there. What had she done? Walked to the supermarket to buy supper? Was there a shopping center near that he didn't know about? It was possible. They kept building new ones every month. He went down the stairs and followed the path to the front gate, meaning to look up and down the street for her. But a window latch clacked and he stopped and turned back. All the windows he could see reflected red sunset light. Except one in the big square room upstairs. That one was wide open and framed in it was Hunsinger. His upper half. The long white hair, white Buffalo Bill moustache, chalk-white skin. He was shirtless.

"We're closed," he called. "Come back tomorrow."

"It's Brandstetter," Dave said. "I have news for Fleur. She wanted me to find Adam Streeter's lawyer and I found him."

"Oh, shit," Hunsinger said, and left the window.

Dave returned to the porch and heard Hunsinger's footfalls thump stairs someplace inside. Or maybe felt them. The porch boards caught the vibrations. Dry rot had probably got into the house supports. Or termites. Or both. Hunsinger appeared framed by the oval glass. He zipped up his ragged Levis and pulled open the door. He still had a partial erection. It was making a damp place in the thin fabric. "God is dead, right?" Dave said.

Hunsinger's white flat cheeks flushed pink. "She's lonely. They buried him today. I was only trying to comfort her."

"She is here, then," Dave said. "Will she come down?"

"Did he leave her any money?" Hunsinger asked.

"I had you all wrong," Dave said, "didn't I? That makes me feel bad." Fleur came through a door beside the tall glass refrigerators. She wore sandals and jeans with earth stains at the knees, and was buttoning a cambric shirt with a sleeve pulled loose at the shoulder. Her face was smooth, impassive, but worry was bright in her eyes. Dave said, "I like to think I know people. It's important in my line of work. I slipped with you. I'm getting old. I'd better quit."

"You're not making sense," Hunsinger said.

Dave said, "You know he left her money. She told you he was going to. This between you isn't new. You've been sleeping together since she lived in the rear house at your place. That was why Adam Streeter moved her out. He suspected, if he didn't know. It wasn't because the neighborhood was dangerous."

"He knew," Fleur said, and came forward to stand next to Hunsinger. His gaunt height made her look even tinier than she was. "I swore to Adam I would stop seeing Hunsinger, and I did stop. We did stop." She took Hunsinger's bony arm in both her small hands and gazed up at him adoringly. "It was very difficult. But Adam was kind and generous to me. I had to obey him. Still, he was upset. And I wondered if, perhaps, after all, there would be anything for me when he died."

Dave said stiffly, "The lawyer's name is Charles Albright." He found Albright's card in his side jacket pocket and held it out to Fleur. "He's out of town right now. You can phone him next week for the particulars. But he authorized me to tell you Streeter left you ten thousand dollars."

Hunsinger yelped, "That won't even pay for the van."

"Darling, don't," Fleur pleaded. "It's all right. It was"—she looked solemnly at Dave—"very generous of him. He was always so thoughtful of me, so protective."

"You were his wife—same as," Hunsinger said. He told Dave, waving his arms, "His live-in companion. I mean, they fucked up there in that bed all the time. Whenever he was in town. He lived here. I can show you his clothes in her closet. She can sue. She should get all the money." He put a skinny arm around her and dragged her hard against him. "She gave him everything. Ten thousand dollars? Shit, man."

Dave said, "Chrissie gets the bulk of the estate. His daughter. She's blind, Hunsinger. You want to go into court to take money away from a blind girl?"

The Adam's apple pumped in Hunsinger's long throat. He flushed pink again. He sulked. "It's not fair," he said.

"You counted on more, didn't you?" Dave said. "Otherwise you'd have dropped her. You certainly wouldn't have waited around practicing chastity. For how long?"

"Three years," Hunsinger grumbled.

"That's a long time," Dave said. "Was it your limit? If so, wasn't it lucky for you he died when he did?" Dave glanced at Fleur. "For both of you?"

"I wasn't waiting for his money," Hunsinger said. "We love each other. He had her trapped by her own sense of gratitude. Making her feel she owed him because he got her out of Cambodia. Tying her up in business debts she could never meet without his help. I wanted to marry her. Did he? Shit, he didn't give a damn for her. All he cared about was himself. He used her like a whore."

"I'm not surprised you weren't at the funeral," Dave said.

"Anybody that was didn't know him." Hunsinger's laugh was sour. "They thought he was the all-American charm-boy, didn't they? And so fucking brave, barging in wherever the bullets were flying." He snorted. "And all the time he's keeping a helpless, bewildered little Cambodian waif his body slave." Hunsinger bent and kissed her forehead. "He was a coward, Brandstetter, a coward and a bully."

"It's over now," Dave said. "Somebody saw to that. Somebody with no higher opinion of him than you." He turned and crossed the porch. At the foot of the steps, he paused and looked back. "Do you happen to own a pair of wire cutters?"

"No," Hunsinger said sharply. "Why would we?"

"In the shed in back," Fleur said.

Dave found them there, on a workbench, beside a big wooden spool of thick smooth wire. They used the wire to fashion hangers for pots with plants in them. Dave picked up the cutters. Scraps of wire lay on the bench. He snipped one in half. Easily. He laid the cutters down, stepped out of the shed into dying daylight, and closed the door behind him.

Leppard's living quarters were at the top of a block-long cement staircase in the hills off Glendale Boulevard. The houses were of old rough gray stucco, with stingy windows. They climbed the hill close on either side of the endless stairs. Dave caught glimpses of women in bright kitchens. Smells and sounds of frying hamburger and onions came out because it was a warm evening and the windows were open. He saw families at supper around K-Mart dining tables, or behind trays in small living rooms where they watched the evening news. Once, pausing to catch his breath, he thought he heard Cecil's voice for a few seconds, but here shutters prevented his seeing a screen. He climbed again, and loud rock music came from a bedroom where a teenage girl in a straw-color ponytail and faded pink exercise tights danced by herself in front of a mirror.

Winded, Dave stood at Leppard's door for a minute before he pushed the bell. Leppard hadn't bought shutters. Roller shades covered his windows, but the evening breeze moved them a little, and light showed around their edges. The familiar voices of newscasters came out to Dave. He didn't try the bell again. He rattled a loose little black knocker in the center of the door. Waited. Rattled it again. And Leppard jerked the door open. Annoyed, and knotting a white towel at his waist. Shaving cream smeared his face, white as the streak in his hair.

"What the fuck—?" he said. Then, "Oh, it's you. What do you want?"

"To correct a mistake," Dave said.

"Come in," Leppard said. "I have a date, and I'm in a hurry." When Dave stepped inside past him, he shut the door again, and crossed the room to a door that was open and showed a bathroom. He picked up a Bic razor there, and standing at a washbasin and gazing into a mirror steamy except for a circle in the middle he'd made with a hand, shaved. "What mistake?" he said, and cranked a faucet. Water splashed.

"I told you I had reason to believe a witness." Dave looked at the small room. The double doors with mirrors to his left plainly held a drop-down bed. An alcove housed a tiny refrigerator and a tiny stove. A cheap fake Oriental carpet covered the floor. There were two meager upholstered chairs and a coffee table. A bridge lamp made of glazed plaster with a white nick in it. Television set on the floor. Nothing else. Except clothes. Leppard had rigged poles along the side of the room, and the poles sagged with clothes enough to stock a small men's store. A very expensive men's store. Some of the clothes were sacked in plastic, but some were not, and the richness of the material and the tailoring were easy to see. "The witness," Dave said, "who told me about the men who came to Underhill's in the early morning."

"The ones in combat camouflage?" The water splashed in the basin again. The razor clicked on the chipped porcelain. Leppard used a blue washcloth to rinse away the lather from his face, dried his face on a towel that hung crooked off a rack, and came out of the bathroom again. He crouched by a stack of orange crates and picked out blue bikini undershorts, stood, let the towel fall, stepped into the shorts. "The ones with the four-by-four, the Bronco with the pintle mount on the roof? It never happened?" Leppard snapped the tight little shorts and grinned mockery at Dave. "You surprise me."

"The witness is sleeping with Streeter's Cambodian girlfriend," Dave said, "for the money he thought Streeter was going to leave her."

Leppard took a shirt down from a hanger on one of the poles, studied it critically, hung it back, chose another, and put it on. "And you think he dreamed up this story about the night raiders so you wouldn't suspect him?"

"It crossed my mind," Dave said.

"But wasn't he trying to get Underhill off?" Leppard sat on a chair and pulled on blue socks. The television newscast ran on without sound. He eyed it for a minute. "And if he did that, wouldn't we start looking for somebody else? And why wouldn't it be him?"

"That too crossed my mind. But add this into the equation. Someone used wire cutters on a fence back of Streeter's condominium—on the night he was killed. Someone who came by water. And I've found only one set of wire cutters. In Fleur's potting shed. Right under Hunsinger's hand."

"Hunsinger?" Leppard studied jackets and slacks on his poles. He turned to blink at Dave. "The hippie who thinks it's still the sixties, the dude who rented the house to Underhill on his back lot? The so-called psychologist?"

"That's the one," Dave said. "He either wanted the bucks Streeter was going to leave to Fleur, or he really did love her and want to marry her. Or both. You can ask him. He claims to have hated Streeter for abusing the girl. And I doubt he can account for his whereabouts the night Streeter died."

"Did he own a Desert Eagle .357 Magnum?"

"Streeter had that in his possession, a drawer in his workroom. Maybe he tried to defend himself with it, and Hunsinger got it away from him and shot him."

"And he got in by cutting that fence and climbing over those condominium roofs?" Leppard looked scornful, and turned back to take down a pair of gray-blue linen slacks and unfasten them carefully from their wooden hanger. He clicked the hanger back on the pole. "That's movietime shit." He held the trousers and, teetering on one leg, then the other, kicked into them. "I told you before."

"It had to be that way," Dave said. "Nobody passed the gate. I asked the security guard, and I believe her."

"Yeah, well"—Leppard zipped the beautiful trousers—"you believed Hunsinger about the commandos, too." From a peg by a closet door, Leppard took down a slim alligator belt, and threaded it through the loops of the slacks. "Hunsinger does dope. Maybe he believes that was what he saw. But that doesn't mean we have to believe it."

"The woman on the gate doesn't do dope," Dave said.

Leppard laughed. "You never know. These little old ladies can fool you. Don't buy a used car from her. She may drag race up on Mulholland Drive on her nights off."

"I had a teenage boy climb over those roofs for me," Dave said. "He did it with ease. From the rear, where the fence was cut. It took him only a few minutes to drop down onto the balcony outside Streeter's workroom."

"Like the captain said—you're thorough." Leppard chose alligator shoes from a rack on the floor and sat in the chair again to put them on. "But I still say it was Underhill. In my book, a hundred thousand large bills beats a piece of ass any time as a motive. Plus, he bought the airline ticket. The commandos didn't plant it on him." Leppard opened a closet and studied neckties arrayed on a wire inside the door. His shirt was electric blue. He took down a tie just a shade or two lighter, edged it under the collar, stood at the Murphy bed door mirrors to give it a big loose knot. "The commandos were a druggie's dream."

On the television set, footage shot from a helicopter showed the white wreckage of a small plane in mountain wilderness, a steep canyon, rocks, pines. Dave bent and turned up the sound. The voice-over spoke of winds, horseback rescue teams, rugged country, delays because of darkness. "The pilot, George McGregor, was wanted for questioning by Los Angeles police in the shooting death of journalist Adam Streeter." Dave felt Leppard come up behind him to stand watching. "McGregor regularly ferried passengers and freight in and out of Mexico and Central America, and figured in two important drug smuggling trials in recent years. The plane carried no passengers, but rescue teams found luggage containing about two hundred fifty thousand dollars in U.S. currency. McGregor's body was—" Leppard switched off the set.

Dave said, "It was true about the deal to buy the Cessna. McGregor told me himself. Came to Underhill's house to get the money while I was there, the other morning."

Leppard went to get a baby-blue jacket off the pole. "But Underhill didn't complete the deal." He put the jacket on.

"You arrested him too soon," Dave said. "Experts will be examining that plane to find out the cause of the crash. Talk to them. You'll find it wasn't an accident."

"Oh, please." Leppard picked up wallet, keys, change from the coffee table, and pushed these into pockets. His Omega was gold, with a gold bracelet. He slipped it onto a thick wrist. "McGregor flew every day of his life. Flying's not like laying in bed, you know. It's risky. The law of averages caught up with him, that's all."

"McGregor was Underhill's only alibi for why he had that money," Dave said. "Whoever framed him for Streeter's murder had to get McGregor out of the way. Surely that's obvious."

"Could Hunsinger do it? Does he know aircraft?"

"I don't know, but he was away from home all day after you arrested Underhill. He could have driven down the coast and tampered with the plane while McGregor was up here looking for Underhill in Venice."

"Not in that van," Leppard said, "not with those tires. How did he know about McGregor and the Cessna deal, anyway?"

"Why didn't Fleur whisper it in his ear? After Streeter whispered it in hers. In the dark. In the very same bed."

"You've got quite a mind." Leppard gave his head a wondering shake, and went around the apartment shutting and locking windows. He opened the front door. "You want to let me go and pick up my lady now?" He switched off the lights.

"McGregor's plane was sabotaged." Dave stepped outside, where not much daylight was left now. Lamps on old-fashioned bronze standards lit the staircase at yellow intervals below. "You can bet the farm on it."

"Not me." Leppard pulled the door shut and used a key to double-lock it. "All I own is clothes."

## 10

It was midnight. Dave sat at his desk in the rear building, no light on in the long, raftered room except here. A mug stood at his elbow. When he tasted the coffee in the mug, it was cold. Cigarette smoke hung in the lamplight. The thick black book lay open in front of him. He had pushed maybe halfway through it, reading each passage Adam Streeter had highlighted in yellow pen, and reading whole pages where the only marker was a slip of paper. He felt gloomy. Reading the sad, bloody history of Los Inocentes would depress anyone, the grisly catalog of butchers like Cortez-Ortiz who had held power there almost from the start. Dave closed the book, rose stiffly from the desk, stretched. The canyon night was quiet. The jangle of the telephone was loud.

"That was a cold lady," Leppard said in his ear. "So I had time on my hands all by myself. And I drove around to talk to Hunsinger, and he wasn't home."

"Did his dog bark at you?"

"Dog wasn't home, either. Big white dog, right?"

"Snowy by name. And not friendly."

"I saw the dog dish in the kitchen," Leppard said, "an empty dog food can in the sink, dog bed in a corner of the bedroom, matted with white hair. Warm day. House was shut up. Smelled of dog, but there wasn't any dog."

"You went through the house," Dave said.

"Like you went through Underhill's," Leppard said. "I'm learning things from you, Mr. Brandstetter. That man is a reading fool. Books stacked all over. Also a writing fool. Never saw so much typing paper with typing already on it."

"Is he writing a book?"

"More like twenty books, it looks like. He's got this theory about why people do what they do. It isn't why they think. They don't know themselves at all. He is into getting us all to know ourselves. When we do that, the world will be paradise, no greed, no crime, nobody seeking power over anyone else, pure water, pure air, love, peace, joy, and vegetarianism. Save the whales, save the muskrats—"

"I wonder you could tear yourself away." Dave turned to look at the bar in deep shadow under the new wing of the sleeping loft. He would like a drink to go with this conversation. Leppard was lonely. Who knew how long he would talk? "Did you learn anything else?"

"That his closet was empty," Leppard said. "He took his clothes and his dog and left. Also twenty-four tea bags— herb tea. The empty box was on a kitchen counter. With the cellophane the box was wrapped in."

"Is marijuana an herb?" Dave said.

"You got me," Leppard said. "So I thought about what you said about that busy bed. The one that belongs to the Cambodian lady. Fleur? And I checked the Yellow Pages and drove by her place. She keeps lights on in the yard, but the house was dark. I pictured her and Hunsinger humping in that bed together, and after what I went through tonight, it put me in a bad mood. I stomped up on that porch and kicked that door. I really wanted to interruptus their coitus."

"When I did that," Dave said, "Hunsinger was not philosophical about it. Did he like it better this time?"

"He wasn't there," Leppard said. "His junky old VW bus was in her driveway, but he wasn't there."

"She's paying for a beautiful lavender van," Dave said, "so new it still has its paper license plates."

"It wasn't there," Leppard said. "She wasn't there. I went inside. Her clothes are missing, too. They took the best vehicle, didn't they, and left together?"

"It's a little early to be sure," Dave said. "But it's interesting. She has ten thousand dollars coming from Adam Streeter's will—so his lawyer tells me."

"Which means you scared her very much," Leppard said.

"Not her." Dave lifted his head. Cecil's van rumbled off Horseshoe Canyon Trail into the brick yard of the front building. Dave told Leppard, "When I asked if they owned wire cutters, Hunsinger jumped to deny it. Fleur just told me calmly where to find them. If he murdered Streeter, I don't think she knows it."

"Then why run away with him?" Leppard said.

"Because she'd believe any excuse he gave her," Dave said. "She's a type you run into sometimes." He saw again the soft change in Fleur's eyes the other morning in Hunsinger's overgrown driveway when Dave had offered to get her the name of Streeter's lawyer from Underhill. "Any man who'll do a kindness for her, she's ready to melt in his arms."

Leppard grunted. "Type you may run into sometimes. Type I run into hates the color blue, and has no use for a man who pays too much attention to his appearance. Man like that is vain and selfish, and probably impotent."

"She didn't want to investigate that?" Dave said.

"No way." Leppard laughed bleakly. "Shit."

"You putting out an APB on Hunsinger and Fleur?" Cecil came in. Dave raised a hand to him and smiled.

Leppard said, "I'll talk it over with the DA in the morning. Maybe he'll want to link them up with Underhill—part of a conspiracy. What do you think?"

"I think Hunsinger cut that fence, which is destruction of private property. There must be a law against that."

"I'm still in Santa Monica," Leppard said. "Don't feel like going home yet. Not far from you. Come out, meet me, and I'll buy you a drink. We can talk it over."

"Sorry," Dave said. "It's past my bedtime."

"Yeah." Leppard sighed. "Sleep well." He hung up.

Cecil cocked an eyebrow and passed the desk, making for the bar. "Somebody trying to date you behind my back?" Dave laughed. The door of the bar refrigerator slapped. A bottle cap was pried off. Cecil emerged from the shadows with a Heineken and a glass. "I'm sorry I was out when you came by the station. I got a mysterious phone call and went to check on it." He stopped beside the desk and looked at Dave. "Oh, excuse me. I thought you already had a drink."

"I'll get it, thanks." Dave went into the shadows and the fresh lumber smell that fell to the bar from the planks above. He rummaged up ice cubes, a glass, the Glenlivet. "How mysterious?" He uncorked the bottle. "Why mysterious?"

"For three reasons." Cecil switched on a lamp at the near end of the long corduroy couch. "First, the caller spoke English so badly I was surprised the switchboard knew who to put the call through to." He sat on the raised hearth, leaned forward, poured the glass full of suds and beer. "Second, he said he had seen me at San Feliz the other night asking who shot the kid in the irrigation ditch." The bottle clinked on the hearth stone. "And third, he could give me the answer."

Dave poured whiskey over the ice cubes and recorked the bottle. "And you had to go to him, because he didn't want to tell you on the phone."

"I told you they were scared to death down there."

"I remember." Dave sipped the whiskey, went to the desk to snap off the lamp and pick up cigarettes and lighter. He carried these to the couch and sat down facing Cecil. "And I don't think you should have gone. To answer this call, I mean. Not without taking me with you."

"You worry too much." Cecil drank some beer. "I'm only a reporter. We don't threaten anybody."

"The truth about a murder does," Dave said. "Where did he say to meet him?"

"A bar called El Borracho. Brooklyn Avenue. The east side. You know the kind of place, blind dirty white stucco front with graffiti, half the letters on the neon sign out of gas, a door that looks like nobody passes through without kicking it a few times first. Greasy curtains inside the door. Bad lighting, air full of smoke and beer fumes, disinfectant smell blowing in from the back hall, the restrooms. Jukebox turned up loud with mariachi music, everybody yelling his head off to be heard over it, laughter, arguments, breaking bottles."

"The Polo Lounge," Dave said.

Cecil grinned. "Something like that."

"I shouldn't joke." Dave lit a cigarette. "You were foolish to go to a place like that alone. Don't do it again, all right?" He waited for Cecil to nod. Cecil didn't nod. He looked stubborn. Dave said, "Was he there?"

"He must have been waiting outside someplace, watching for me to show up. He came in afterward. He knew who to look for. I didn't. I was standing, wondering how to get through the crowd to the bar when he bumped me, and when I looked at him he smiled. Now, there were only men in this place, but it was no gay bar. So I figured this must be him, little guy, brown leathery skin, gray hair, bad teeth, funny pale blue eyes. He knew how to get to the bar, and he brought back draft beers and led me out back to the alley.

"It was dark out there. Somebody was throwing up. When he got through and staggered back inside, this ragged little dude, Porfirio, told me it was gringos who shot the kid—gringos in jungle fatigues and combat boots and berets, all right? They roared up to the irrigation canal in a Cherokee, dragged the kid out, bound and gagged, forced him to his knees in the reeds, and shot him point-blank through the head. Then they yanked the gag out and untied his hands, and dumped his body into the water. They scrambled back into the four-by-four and tore off out of there. People in the shacks heard the shot—it woke them up. But Porfirio was the only one who saw. He was taking a bath in the ditch, under a bridge, where he could hang his clothes and put his soap and towel. The plumbing is kind of primitive down there. He was so close to these killers, he pissed, thinking they'd seen him."

"Why didn't he tell the police when they came?"

"I asked him the same thing." Cecil drank off the beer in the glass, and poured what was left in the bottle into the glass, watching it foam. "Maybe he's more than an illegal. He could be a fugitive. He just said you don't talk to law enforcement types if you can't show them a green card. And he didn't tell anyone until he learned the kid was from Los Inocentes. That's unusual in San Feliz. And no one in San Feliz is political. They're refugees from hunger, that's all. And Porfirio heard that this kid was political, frightened, hiding out. So he thought he'd better tell somebody. And he chose me."

"And does he know who the death squad were?"

Cecil gave his head a glum shake. "Here we get into folklore. There's this mythic character, El Coronel, okay? No one knows who he is, but he's said to have a secret army hidden in the mountains. The man who started the legend was named Tamayo. His old car broke down back of nowhere, he went for help, got lost, and stumbled on these young Latinos dressed like Vietnam grunts in some dusty canyon. Guns, grenades, the works. Some of them were running hunched over up a creek bed, and the rest were shooting at them from the trees."

"And Tamayo," Dave said, "isn't around anymore—right?"

"Right. Like your flying dude, McGregor," Cecil said. "His plane crashed. Did you see it on the news?"

"It's bad news for Underhill." Dave smoked, frowning into the shadows. "Will Porfirio let you put him on TV?"

"Hell, no. And even if he would, I couldn't, could I? I mean, who knows if what he says is true? He can't prove it. He was alone in that canal. But if I need him, I have his address—nineteen twenty-two City View. And he's got my phone number."

Dave grunted, drank whiskey, tapped ash off his cigarette. "Why the hell did Hunsinger run?"

"Say what?" Cecil said. He rose and reached for Dave's glass, in which only ice remained. He went away into the tall darkness. While Dave outlined for him what he had learned about Hunsinger today, Cecil made the Glenlivet bottle gurgle, its cork squeak going back into place. He got himself another Heineken from the little refrigerator, and brought bottle and Scotch glass back into the light. He put the glass into Dave's hand. Dave said, "Thank you," and wound up the Hunsinger log, "But now, with this story of Porfirio's, I wonder if Hunsinger wasn't telling the truth, after all."

"About the midnight visitors to Underhill's?"

"The description jibes." Dave drank, set the glass under the lamp, stubbed out his cigarette, lit another, and scowled at Cecil through the smoke. "And the dead boy was from Los Inocentes. Among all those Mexican farm workers. Hiding out. Frightened. And Streeter was running. Frightened. By something he'd learned for his story about Los Inocentes—the newsbreak of the decade. You don't suppose—"

"I don't suppose it was this dead boy Streeter went to interview on that long drive he took he wouldn't tell Chrissie about? I don't suppose the boy knew who had kidnapped Cortez-Ortiz, and told Streeter the name, and got killed for telling? Is that what you're asking?"

"You understand me so well." Dave coaxed him with a smile. "Why aren't we working together anymore?"

"Seems to me we are." Cecil filled his glass again. "I saw Dr. Scheinwald at County USC Medical Center, like I promised. And there wasn't any need to drive to Sierra Madre to find the Tom Fraser family. They were right there at the hospital—mother and daughter, anyway. Excuse me." He rose, and left the lamplight again, this time to cross the wide room. A door closed. After a minute, a toilet flushed. Water ran in the pipes. The door opened. Cecil came back into the light, sat down, took another gulp of beer.

"Your attachment to dramatic pauses is getting out of hand," Dave said. "What about Glendenning's alibi?"

"Whose what?" Cecil looked bewildered. "Oh, that. He was there with them, just the way he said—all night."

"Thank you. That's nice to know." Dave frowned at the telephone on the dark desk. "I wonder why Ray Lollard hasn't got back to me with a location on that phone number I found at Underhill's. And an up-to-date list of Streeter's call-outs. Ray never kept me waiting before."

"You're never home," Cecil said, "and you always forget to activate the answering machine."

"I don't forget. It's deliberate." Dave drank the last of his whiskey. "Irrational, but deliberate." He moved the glass in a circle, listening to the ice rattle. "I'll phone him in the morning."

"You want to know," Cecil said, "whether Streeter rang somebody in San Feliz?"

"Somebody named Rafael," Dave said. "Ray told me the number was down among the big produce ranches."

"Dave, I can't drive all the way to San Feliz to ask if anybody saw Streeter there the night the boy was killed. It would take the best part of a day. Donaldson won't give me the time. Everybody's on vacation. I'm already working double shifts. You know that."

Dave put out his cigarette. "You ready for bed?"

Cecil sighed. "I thought you'd never ask."

## 11

FLAT LAND STRETCHED away in every direction to mountains three inches high on the horizon. The earth was yellow-brown, striped with green rows of lettuce, cabbage, cauliflower. Sealed in the air-conditioned Jaguar, Dave smelled the crops, especially the onions when he passed onion fields. The wheels of the Jaguar rattled the rough planks of bridges across irrigation canals. The sluggish water in these ditches mirrored a hard hot sky the blue of steel. Now and then a trail of dust far off across a field showed where a truck carried crates of harvested produce, or piles of empty crates, or a crowd of brown-skinned field hands in ragged straw hats, dusty coveralls, cracked shoes, men, women, children. He saw other workers, stooped, laboring in the fields. Or gathered around an old tanker truck for water to drink.

San Feliz was a loose scatter of buildings, stucco over frame mostly, some stucco over cement block, some sun-bleached yellow brick. Clumps of pepper trees and ragged-barked eucalyptus trees shadowed them. There were big old date palms sometimes. The shops sold hardware, groceries, clothes. A single bank occupied a corner. The lone motel called itself the Rest E-Z. A middle-aged woman, scrawny in walking shorts and a halter, was turning a garden hose on plantings in front of the straw-color motel units, but the petunias there were wilting anyway. Ed's Oasis was a tavern in a gaunt frame building whose jigsaw decorations where spooled supports met porch roofs had cracked in the dry heat of decades and sections fallen away. Pickup trucks stood in front of the place, a lumbering Cadillac, rickety RVs, a sports car. Dust coated them all. Dave was thirsty, but he drove past.

The settlement of Mexican field hands was a mile beyond San Feliz itself. He crossed a canal bridge to a cluster of twenty scaly stucco shacks long ago painted bright pink, yellow, purple. The paint had flaked away in patches. Iron pipes with faucets stuck up out of the ground beside the doors of the shacks. The faucets dripped. Little brown kids played in the puddles, squatting, muddying their diapers—those that wore diapers. Chickens pecked in the dust. Flies buzzed. From the open windows of one shack drifted thin radio music—marimba, accordion, guitars. Somewhere, a goat bleated.

A fat grandmother sat on a doorstep watching the children, her eyes milky with cataracts. A thin grandmother without teeth leaned in a doorway, bony arms crossed, staring out at the fields. One who might have been her sister sat on a broken kitchen chair under a dusty oleander heavy with pink flowers, and fanned herself with a tattered magazine. In the shade at the side of one shack, a skin-and-bones old man lay on a rusty tube-and-webbing lawn chaise beside a stack of gray, threadbare automobile tires. A cheap cotton blanket covered him to the chest. A Gatorade jar filled with water stood in dry weeds beside the cot. Back of the same house, a very pregnant young woman bent over a green plastic laundry basket, lifted wet clothes from it, pinned them to a sagging wire. Dave stopped the Jaguar, waited for the dust it had raised to settle, then got out of the car. The heat was stunning. He shed his jacket, laid it over the seatback, picked up the book Dan'l had given him the other morning, closed the car door, and went to talk to the girl.

"My name is Brandstetter," he said in Spanish, and held the book out. It was a collection of Adam Streeter's newspaper and magazine pieces, including the one that had got him a Pulitzer Prize three years ago. Streeter's picture was on the back. "I am an insurance investigator. This man"—he tapped the picture—"was insured by my company. He was killed, no one knows by whom. Shot with a gun. I am trying to trace his actions on that day. Did you ever see him here?"

She tilted her head at Dave, a child's red romper suit dripping in her hands. Her brown eyes looked wryly amused. "A famous man who wrote books? What would he be doing in a place like this?" She turned and pinned the romper suit to the clothes wire. "Who would come here who does not have to?"

"He was a journalist, a reporter," Dave said, and smiled slightly. "So he must have been looking for a story to write, don't you think? Are there no stories to write in San Feliz?"

Her laugh was dry and brief, the look in those large, luminous eyes a little scornful. "There are many stories—but not that would interest people like him, people like you. We grow hungry and we eat." With a soft grunt because of the child large in her belly, she bent to lift another bright garment from the basket. She was barefoot, and her feet were grimy. "We get up in the morning before it is light, and climb into trucks, and go to the field and work until it is dark, and come home tired. And we go to bed. Children are born, and old people die." She turned from pinning the thin orange blouse to the line, and glanced along the side of the house to where the old man lay, eyes shut, but not asleep. In pain. "And when there are no more crops to gather, we move on. It is"—she sighed and wiped her chubby brown hands on her faded blue wrap-around skirt—"always the same, perhaps uninteresting, even to us. But it is life." She laid a hand on her swollen belly and smiled down at it—not sentimentally, but thoughtfully. "It is our gift from God."

"How soon will your child be born?" Dave asked.

"Soon." She scrabbled clothespins out of a rumpled pink plastic sack in a corner of the basket, and dropped them into a pocket of the skirt. "That is the reason I am here, and not out in the fields today. But no—I do not know this writer of books. I never saw him." Bending again over the green basket, she waved a hand. "You would do better to ask the old women. They have nothing to do but see who comes and goes."

"The old see only what is past," Dave said. "What about the young man who was shot and his body put into the irrigation ditch? That was no ordinary happening. Did you know that boy? Did you know his name?"

Fear showed in her eyes. She opened them wide for an instant and quickly shook her head. "No, no. I know nothing about that. No one here knew him. He was a stranger."

"Somebody fed him," Dave said, "he slept somewhere."

"*Sí*. But not I." Her hands moved nervously. "Not my family. We did not know him."

"Rafael," Dave said. "Was that his name? I have it on a slip of paper written by Adam Streeter. I am told by the telephone company that Streeter talked to him down here."

She glanced around her, pale, searching the empty, sleepy settlement for a sign of anyone listening. Crows cawed in the distance. The goat bleated again. A child cried. The grandmother with the magazine had dropped it. She slept, chin on bony chest. "*Sí*, Rafael," the young woman whispered. "Why did they kill him? Why did he try to hide here?"

"From the death squad of El Coronel?"

"From the immigration," she said. "They do not want refugees from Los Inocentes in this country."

"But did you hear that it was El Coronel's commandos who shot him?"

She shrugged impatiently. "It is talk, nothing more."

"Were the people he stayed with"—Dave pushed his hair back, and his hand came away damp—"from Los Inocentes also?" The glare was harsh. He narrowed his eyes and looked around at the lonely buildings. "Where can I find them?"

"They are no longer here." Her motions, pinning up the clothes, had become quick, jerky. "They departed that night. Immigration thinks they are all communists. Please, *señor,* I must finish with these clothes. I must lie down, for the sake of my baby." She glanced at the motionless old man again. "I must take my father his medication."

"Why is he not in a hospital?" Dave said.

"They can do nothing. He is dying. He asked to die at home." Her laugh was joyless. "This is the only home he has."

"Will you name the baby for him?" Dave said.

"*Sí,*" she said, and smiled. "Victorio."

"That is a fine name," Dave said, and went back to the car. He tossed the book inside, but before he got in after it, he looked at the frayed wires that hung limply from thin poles in a crooked row behind the shacks. Power lines. No one had a telephone out here. He tossed the jacket into the rear seat, sat behind the Jaguar's leather-wrapped wheel, slammed the door, started the engine. The air from the dashboard jets blew on his sweat-soaked shirt. He swung the heavy car around and, careful to avoid children and chickens, headed back toward the bridge of rusty-bolted beams and planks across the irrigation ditch. There, on a pole beside the bridge, a helmet-shaped blue transparent plastic covering housed a telephone. He stopped the car, reached into the back for his jacket and the reading glasses tucked into it, got out of the car, and stepped to read the number on the pay phone above its rows of steely pushbuttons. This was the pay phone Ray had told him about this morning. Adam Streeter had rung this number not once but three times in the two days before his death. Dave put the glasses into his shirt pocket and stood on the bank looking down at the tall reeds growing in the murky water. Shadows lurked under the bridge, where Porfirio had brought his soap and towel that ugly night to have a bath.

Dave started to turn back to the Jaguar and the wheels of a car rattled the planks of the bridge, and he looked that way. A brown and white cruiser came across the bridge. Its roof held a silvery siren housing and a row of blinker lights white, red, amber. A buggy-whip antenna waved at the rear of the car. A gold star was painted on the front door, along with the words *County Sheriff's Dept.* A hand waved to him from the window on the driver's side. Dave stood and waited until the car braked beside him, its bumper against his bumper. The driver had a square red middle-aged face and wore a flat-brimmed hat with four dents molded into the crown. He turned off the cruiser's engine, pushed the door handle, swung the door open, and climbed out. A young man sat on the passenger side, wearing suntans like his partner's, same sort of hat, badge, gun, sunglasses. He stared ahead, indifferent. The older man's smile didn't mean anything.

"Looks like you're lost," he said. "Away out of your bailiwick. I mean—we don't get cars like that down here in redneck country." His bloodshot blue eyes looked Dave up and down. "We don't get people like you." His gaze flickered away to the cluster of sad, gaily painted shacks. "Specially not out here. You're the wrong color. And you weren't born speaking Spanish. You want to explain your business here?"

Dave showed his license. "I'm on a case for Banner Life. The death of Adam Streeter. At the marina in Los Angeles, a few nights back. He was shot in the head at close range. He was a journalist, working on a story about Los Inocentes. I'm wondering if there was a connection between his death and that of a young man from Los Inocentes shot the same way down here that same night. You solved that case yet?"

"Nope." The deputy watched Dave carefully, spoke carefully. "But that was a family fight. He was holed up with a man and wife from Los Inocentes—brother and sister-in-law, maybe. Nobody knew much about them. But they sure as hell got out of here fast when it happened. And we can't locate them. Not so far. Probably never will. Probably home by now."

"Who says it was a family fight?" Dave asked.

The man shrugged. "Educated guess. Nobody here knew any of them. Who else was there to fight with? It's relatives do most of the killing in this world—not strangers." Sweat darkened the sides of his starchily creased shirt. He took off his hat, mopped a bald head with a handkerchief, pushed the handkerchief back into his hip pocket. "Isn't it farfetched to connect a murder up in LA to one way down here? Writing about Los Inocentes? Isn't everybody, these days?"

"I think he drove down here to get information from the boy." Dave got the book from the car, showed the deputy Streeter's picture. "You didn't see him in this vicinity? Low-slung black sports car?" Dave jerked his head at the telephone. "He had this phone number. He'd completed calls to it three times."

"I never saw him." The deputy passed the book back.

"There's more." The jacket of the book was wet from the deputy's hand. "A witness I talked to saw troops in combat fatigues and berets late that night near the house of Streeter's assistant. So, when a witness turns up who says troops of that description came to this place and shot this young man, Rafael, and dumped him in the canal, it—" Dave looked into the deputy's red, dumbfounded face. "You didn't hear about that? No one said anything to you about El Coronel's men coming and executing that boy? Right here where we're standing?"

"Oh, bullshit." The deputy blustered, but he was faking. He looked sick. "That El Coronel stuff is a marijuana pipe dream. These are ignorant people, Mr. Bannerman, no schooling, primitive, childish. They tell stories like that to scare themselves." He laughed. He stopped laughing. "How did you know his name? What was it—Rafael?"

"It was written beside this telephone number on Streeter's scratch pad. This witness told a friend of mine that he was right here under this bridge, taking a bath, when El Coronel's death squad brought the kid in a Cherokee, gagged and bound, shot him, and dumped him in the canal. He saw the whole thing."

"Come on!" The youngster in the car showed some life at last. He scrambled out, and came around the car in long strides, scowling. "Why didn't he tell me, then? I was here in this patrol car ten minutes after the thing happened, and nobody saw nothing. They was all inside, asleep, the way they told it. Who was this witness? Where do I find him?"

"Nineteen twenty-two City View, Boyle Heights," Dave said. "He didn't speak up because he hasn't any green card. He was afraid you'd turn him over to Immigration and he'd be deported. But he had to tell somebody. He'd seen my friend down here, a television reporter, asking questions, and he took a Greyhound up to LA and contacted him. El Coronel and his hired guns are sure as hell real enough to him."

The older deputy made a face. "Who is this witness?"

"This TV reporter that tall black kid?" asked the young deputy. "Channel Three, LA? He sure can get in the way of police investigation. Give a jig a little education, and right away he starts walking all over everybody."

"Redneck country, did you say?" Dave asked the older man.

He swelled up. "Just give me this witness's name."

"He calls himself Porfirio," Dave said.

"That old drunk?" The boy deputy laughed and wagged his head. "Shit—you believe him? His brain is pickled in Coors, man. Passes out in the street. We didn't pick him up and take him to jail, the trucks would run over him."

"You say he was taking a bath?" the older deputy asked. "Hell—Porfirio hasn't taken a bath in ten years. Get downwind of him next time, you'll see." He turned for the car, plunked himself solidly inside, slammed the door. "You don't want to believe everything you hear, Mr. Bannerman." He started the car's rattly engine. "Not when it's Mexicans talking." He scraped the gears. "And Porfirio does have a green card." The deputy poked his head out the window and twisted it on its thick neck so he could pilot the car backward across the thumping planks of the bridge. "He must have the first one they ever printed. Porfirio?" He laughed as if it was the funniest thing he'd heard in a long time.

## 12

CITY VIEW WAS a street of little frame houses along a low ridge. Dave hadn't been in this part of LA for thirty years, maybe longer, and he was shocked. He remembered it as poor but neat. Jews had lived here then. A generation of Jewish kids had grown up on these look-alike streets with their pinched look-alike houses. He knew some of those kids—Abe Greenglass, his lawyer, was one. They'd prospered and were living out their old age in handsome west side apartments or ranch houses on broad lawns in Van Nuys and Sherman Oaks. They remembered poverty, or thought they did. They didn't. Boyle Heights had gone from ghetto to barrio. Now there was poverty—not the kind anyone would romanticize from the comfort of wealthy suburbs. Real poverty.

The houses needed paint. Roofing had weathered through to the tar and the tar was faded gray by rain, sun, wind. Chimneys had lost bricks in earthquakes or from the simple shifting of the land under skimpy foundations. TV aerials had toppled. Broken windowpanes were mended with stained cardboard. Once grass had grown in the grudging front yards—now they were bare yellow hard-pan. Old auto chassis on wheels stripped of tires gathered grime in short, steep driveways. Cars in not much better shape rusted at the curbs, their dusty windows glaring red in the sunset light. The porch of number nineteen twenty-two had pulled away some from the house and looked ready to slide downhill.

Dave stood for a moment at the foot of the cracked cement steps and looked along the street both ways. A pair of men, one squat, one tall, stood at a far corner. Cowboy boots, crimp-brimmed straw hats. But no Cherokee, Blazer, Bronco with black glass and a pintle mount on the roof was anywhere in sight. Dave climbed the steps to a cracked cement footpath, went up the footpath, and halted to test the wooden front porch steps gingerly with a foot. They hung at an odd angle, askew, like a stroke victim's mouth, but they didn't creak or wobble, and he climbed them. The gap between the front wall of the house and the porch where it had pulled away and showed rusty spikes was maybe nine inches, maybe a foot. He reached across and used knuckles on the frame of a torn screen door. The solid door inside it stood open. Radio or television talk came out. In Spanish. The door was loose, and gave a satisfying rattle. He was heard.

A woman came, small, her brown skin webbed with wrinkles, hair pulled tightly back and knotted, eyes black as basalt. She studied him, head turned a little aside, distrustful.

He told her who he was, lying again about Banner Life, and said in Spanish that it was urgent that he talk to Porfirio. The young black to whom Porfirio had spoken about events in San Feliz was a mutual friend. The woman narrowed her eyes and said nothing. Dave said, "It is now known in San Feliz that Porfirio told the young black man the facts about an evil thing that happened there the other night."

"There is no one of that name here," the woman said, and shook her head, her mouth a firm line of denial. But something made her look over her shoulder. There was no light in the house behind her, but Dave wondered if he didn't see someone there, a boy or a small man, framed in a doorway. The woman began to swing the front door closed. "You have made a mistake. You have come to the wrong house."

Dave said loudly, "He could be in grave danger. I gave this address to the San Feliz sheriff. I think he may have warned El Coronel. His death squad could come here at any moment to kill Porfirio."

"Why?" Porfirio said this. He thrust the woman aside. The door swung back and banged a wall. He pushed the screen door open and glared with those strange pale blue eyes at Dave. His clothes were ragged, his gray hair uncombed, white stubble on his chin. "Why did you tell them this address?"

"On the chance that they would contact El Coronel— and they did make an urgent telephone call from Ed's Oasis only a few minutes after I talked to them. If El Coronel's death squad killed young Rafael, I believe they will come here."

"You made me bait in a trap," Porfirio said. He looked sick. "I should never have told. I knew that. But honor would not let me keep silent." He grabbed Dave's sleeve with hands that trembled. "And now I will die." His breath reeked of beer. Tears leaked down the dirty furrows of his face. "How could you do such a thing to me? Have I ever harmed you? We are strangers."

"Get your clothes," Dave said. "I will take you away from here. If they come, they will not find you. All I need is to know who they are for myself." He turned the bony little man and gave him a light push. "Quickly, now. Waste no time." The woman stood back watching, face impassive, lumpy body tense, hands clenched. Dave stepped into the house. It smelled of supper cooking—chilis, onions, pinto beans. Fine, dark, rich smells. His mouth watered. He hadn't eaten all day. He took the woman's hand, folded a fifty-dollar bill into it, and said, "I will send Porfirio away and come back. Should these gringos come, tell them you

117

expect Porfirio at any moment. Keep them waiting until I return."

She looked at the bill, at the street, and gave him a tight, frightened nod. "But you must return, *señor*. If you do not return, they will kill me for lying to them. That is the way of death squads."

"I'll be back." Dave read his watch. The hour alarmed him. "Porfirio," he shouted into the darkness of the house. "Stop wasting time. We must get out of here."

The little man appeared carrying a cardboard carton.

When they walked into the coldly lighted, brick-walled Trailways station at eighteen past six, a voice from loudspeakers was caroming around, scrambling the names of towns the next bus out would stop at. This was the final boarding call. The side doors stood open, and a few stragglers were lined up there, weary-looking women, mostly, Latinas, Asians, poor whites with babies, toddlers, bundles. While Dave waited at the counter for a brisk young black woman to fix up Porfirio's ticket, he looked around for a squat man and a tall man in straw hats and cowboy boots. No sign of them. He urged Porfirio across the cigarette- stubbed floor and out into the chugging rumble of the waiting bus. The little man stood as if stunned at the foot of the bus steps until the glum young driver pulled from his hand the ticket Dave had put there. Dave helped Porfirio up into the bus, wanting a look at the other passengers. But the aisle was too busy. He handed Porfirio his carton of clothes, and tucked money into the pocket of his sweaty red-cotton-plaid shirt.

"Guadalupe, right? Your sister's house. Rosa Ramirez, number seven-oh-two Arenoso? Good. Now, stay there, Porfirio. Don't see anyone. People talk, and talk travels. Don't show your face until you hear from me that it's safe."

Porfirio nodded dumbly. Had he heard?

"Can you put it on a postcard?" the driver said to Dave.

"Will it ever be safe?" Porfirio said.

"When El Coronel is in jail," Dave said.

"*Sí.*" Porfirio laughed bleakly. "Tomorrow, yes?"

"Come on, dad, move it," the driver told Dave.

Dave moved it. He waited, leaning against the wall, smoking, eyes searching the dark tinted windows of the bus, wondering who would be traveling with Porfirio. Dave stayed until the luggage was stored in the compartments under the bus and the doors were slammed down, until the driver climbed up and settled himself at the wheel, the passenger doors wheezed shut, the brakes of the bus hissed on being released, and the bus moved with a roar and gusts of smoky exhaust toward the street. Dave made out Porfirio's face at the window. The odd blue eyes watched him, full of dread and resignation.

"He will be all right," Dave told the woman. They sat at a kitchen table where accumulated bottles of hot sauce, jars and cans of jalapenos, containers of spices, bunches of onions, garlic, dried peppers left just enough room for two to put plates and eat. "If you do not tell them where he has gone, and I do not tell them, they will not find him."

"This sister of his"—the woman cautiously peeled corn-husks from around a fat tamale she had made herself—"is my sister also. She has a knife blade for a tongue. She has no use for those who drink. She is one of these born-again Christians. She will make life miserable for him."

Dave husked his own tamale. The smell of it was so good he shut his eyes and simply breathed it in deeply for a minute. Tamales like this he thought had ceased to exist. When he was a kid, he could buy them off a rattly truck that parked under an old pepper tree in the schoolyard at noon. Steaming. For a dime. The same brand could be bought in supermarkets now. But the cornhusk wrappings had been replaced by plastic, and the shredded beef by something called textured vegetable protein. Even the masa meal was tasteless. This was wonderful. So were the pinto beans. So was the rice. He never wanted to eat anywhere else except this dim little kitchen with its crooked cupboard doors, faucet dripping in the sink, scuffed linoleum, faded pink paint. He told the woman:

"He will not have to stay there long." He smiled and wiped his mouth with the small, rough paper napkin she had laid beside his plate. "You are a wonderful cook, *señora.*"

She smiled. Her teeth were discolored, those she still had. But dimples appeared in her withered cheeks, and for a moment it was possible to see the pretty girl she once was. *"Gracias,"* she said, "but it is very unremarkable food."

"Not to me," Dave said. "You do not like the wine?"

He had stopped for a bottle on the way back and paid well for it. Had this been a mistake? It was red, but it lacked roughness. It was not *vino tinto ordinario,* was it? We like what we're used to. But the woman caressed the slim bottle that glinted in the light of a weak bulb dangling from a frayed cord over the table. And smiled again. "It is a lovely wine." Her fingers were small and gnarled on the dark glass. "I thought that I would put the rest away for another time. When the danger is past and we can celebrate."

"It will not keep well," Dave said, and filled her glass again. "I will bring another bottle for that occasion."

"You do not think it will be soon?" She tasted the wine.

"I'm going to try to make it soon," Dave said.

But time stretched out. He helped the woman wash up and put the leftover food away in a gray refrigerator. She tugged a grubby cotton string to turn the light off, and the two of them sat in the small living room on old overstuffed chairs and looked at television while a candle flickered in front of a chipped statuette of the Virgin in a corner. Dave went out to the street every time commercials came on, and looked for the four-by-four vehicle, and climbed back up the sloping porch stairs and stepped across the gap and sat down in the living room again.

The woman brought him a dark brown bottle of Dos Equis, a bowl of tortilla chips, a bowl of cold refried beans, and set these on a low table. This was at ten o'clock. He had begun to feel foolish. By eleven, when nothing had happened, and the woman had fallen asleep in the chair, head back, gently snoring, he began to wonder if Leppard might be right.

Dave had phoned him on the way here. Leppard refused to help. "You've got this death squad craziness on the brain. Hunsinger denies he told you anything about any death squad."

"I have a witness that he did," Dave said. "Where did you find Hunsinger?"

"In Oxnard, on my APB, and they're locked up here. He and Fleur. Conspiracy. Grand theft. With Underhill. The DA thinks Hunsinger found out Underhill meant to skip with Streeter's hundred thousand, and he told Fleur, and Fleur threatened to tell Streeter unless Underhill split the money with her and Hunsinger. Underhill laughed at her, she told Streeter, he demanded his money back, and Underhill shot him."

"What about those wire cutters?" Dave said.

"That section of the fence was junked when they repaired it. No way to compare the cuts with any clippers."

"And the gun?" Dave said.

"You know about the gun, and if you'd told me, it would have saved this department time and money. The gun belonged to a Reverend Pierce Glendenning in Sierra Madre. He thought you sent me. When I said you hadn't, he wept in gratitude. I am not weeping in gratitude, Mr. Brandstetter. What else do you know about this case you haven't told me?"

"You don't like what I do tell you," Dave said, and hung up.

He came indoors again at five past eleven, went to the kitchen for another Dos Equis, came back into the living room to switch channels on the television set and move the bent, corroded antennae to sharpen the picture. He sat down, drank beer, dipped taco chips into the spicy beans and munched them, and watched the Channel

Three news, hoping for a glimpse of Cecil. He hoped also for fresh word on the disappearance of General Cortez-Ortiz from the Guatemalan embassy in Tegucigalpa. File film showed Cortez-Ortiz playing with a dog in a white-walled patio filled with flowering shrubs. The dog was a young Doberman, full of energy and awkwardness. He and the general both had white, menacing teeth, and laughed a lot. But the whereabouts of the general was still a mystery. And Cecil did not show up on camera.

He showed up in person, at midnight, when a rerun of *Vegas* broke for commercials and Dave pushed up wearily out of the butt-sprung overstuffed chair to go out to the silent street under its greenish lamps to look for danger one more time. When he had picked his way down the slumping porch steps, a car's headlights caught his attention, boring along toward this place. A taxicab halted at the curb, and Cecil jumped out. He raised a hand to Dave, leaned in at the window to pay the driver, and turned to regard Dave with strained patience as Dave came down the cement steps to the sidewalk. "What the hell is this?" he said.

"I told you on the phone. When I walked into Ed's Oasis for a beer after the sheriff interviewed me out by the irrigation canal, he was back of the bar, talking on the telephone. In an undertone. Upset and urgent, cupping the mouthpiece with his hand, looking over his shoulder every few seconds. Something was making him sweat. And he was warning somebody about something."

"That the word was out on who killed Rafael?" Cecil looked up and down the deserted street, no lights at any of the windows now, except those at nineteen twenty-two, and everybody asleep. He looked at nineteen twenty-two, the collapsing porch. "You think he was warning El Coronel himself? Yeah. That's why you're here. You told him where to find Porfirio. To flush them out, right? Only now you have to keep Porfirio from being killed. So this is your new permanent address, right?"

"Porfirio is on a bus to Guadalupe," Dave said. He held his watch close to his face. "Should be there by now. His sister's house. To hide until the danger's over."

"But you want a look at who comes to kill him?"

"That's it." Dave nodded. "Me or someone I trust."

"Not the police, Leppard, Ken Barker?"

"Barker's in London," Dave said, "and Leppard has a new homicide. Anyway, he thinks I'm fantasizing." Dave summed up his conversation with Leppard. "So that leaves me on my own. Unless you want to help."

"I'm in the news business now," Cecil said, "remember? Dave, come home."

Dave shook his head. "I have to know who these people are. But I'm tired. I've been up since dawn. I've driven three hundred miles today. And I need you to spell me."

"We have an agreement," Cecil said. "I'm through with shooting and being shot, right? If these dudes don't find Porfirio here, why won't they shoot us? You want to watch them shoot me? You want me to watch them shoot you?"

"They won't do that. We're not witnesses to anything."

"Do you think they'll wait for us to explain that? Come on home." Cecil reached for Dave, but Dave stepped back. "Dave, why are you doing this? You're not getting paid. Lovejoy called you off the case. You want the truth? You're compulsive. You can't leave it alone. You're like Adam Streeter, you know that? You live for danger."

"I live for justice," Dave said.

"Justice is a dream," Cecil scoffed, "a romantic ideal. Who the fuck gets justice in this life? The people living on this street?" His laugh was angry. "Or shall we consider the black people in this country? What the hell did they do?" Tears were in his eyes. His voice trembled. "They didn't even want to come here, for Christ sake."

"Easy," Dave said. "You go on home and sleep now. Forget about this. You're right—it's not your worry."

"Sleep? Without you there? Be serious. That's why I left my van at work and came in a taxi. So we'd have to ride home together. In the Jaguar. Now."

"Sorry." Dave laid the keys in Cecil's hand. "You go along. I'll ring you in the morning."

"Some cop will ring me, to say you're dead. Shit. I wish I'd never taken that call from Porfirio, never come down here in the first place. If it hadn't been for me—"

A car squealed to a halt at the curb. A glossy red sports car. Jeff Leppard climbed out. So clothes were not all he owned. The slam of the car door was loud in the midnight silence. "The commandos show up yet?" He came to them, stocky, sleek. "I didn't think so. And they won't. But I'll stay and see. If you still want."

"I still want," Dave said. "Just to know who they are."

"That's what I'll find out," Leppard said. "Nothing else to do tonight."

"Another ice princess?" Dave asked.

"Same one," Leppard said wanly. "I'm a slow learner."

"You're also a bad liar." Dave studied him. "I was fantasizing when we talked on the phone. You were so sure of that, you almost convinced me. What turned you around?"

"Yeah, well"—Leppard shifted uncomfortably from foot to foot—"I apologize for the way I talked. I was busy."

"This visit isn't an act of contrition," Dave said.

"Not really." Leppard sighed. "After you hung up, the FAA lab called. The rods to the rudder and tail flaps on McGregor's plane had been sawed almost through. Which is why they broke, and why he crashed." Leppard glowered. "But that doesn't mean commandos did it."

"Doesn't mean they didn't," Dave said.

"It could have been Hunsinger," Leppard said.

"Not in that van," Dave said, "not with those tires."

"Why didn't he use Fleur's van?"

"Because she was driving it that day. I saw her."

"Ah, look," Leppard said, "I don't know who sabotaged that plane, but somebody did, and that's why I'm here—

because you keep being right about crazy things, and it makes me nervous."

"This is Cecil Harris," Dave said. "Jeff Leppard."

They shook hands. Leppard looked around him. Over the crooked roofs of the small dark houses, a faint colored haze tinted the sky from signs along a distant business street. Leppard looked at nineteen twenty-two. "Your man Porfirio in there?"

"His sister," Dave said. "I sent him out of town. Out of danger."

"Danger." Leppard snorted and shook his head. "A death squad? In Boyle Heights?"

"You'll see," Dave said.

## 13

CECIL SLEPT, BUT Dave couldn't manage that. At last, he slipped out of bed quietly so as not to disturb Cecil, pushed wearily into a big, loose kimono of brown raw silk, and went softly downstairs. He switched on a lamp by the couch, went to the bar for a squat bottle of Remy Martin and a snifter, and paused at the desk. The black book lay there like a grave marker. He sighed, slid open a desk drawer for an extra pair of reading glasses he kept there, put the glasses on, tucked the book under his arm, returned to the couch. He sat to tilt brandy into the snifter, tasted the brandy, set bottle and glass under the lamp, and stretched out with the book. When he opened it and tried to read, he discovered that the lenses were dusty. With a corner of the robe, he wiped them, set them on his nose again, and read yet again about Lothrop Zorn, Colonel, U.S. Marine Corps, retired.

Zorn's picture accompanied the article. Not a clear picture, reproduced secondhand from a newspaper. The man looked gaunt. A bad writer would say his sunken eyes burned like a fanatic's. Zorn had distinguished himself in Vietnam, returned to the States in 1973, and made no news until 1981, when he was summoned to the White

House as a military adviser on Central America. Before the end of the year, he was down there, El Salvador, Honduras, Los Inocentes, as the President's liaison to the armed forces of those countries. Washington believed the rebels there were being armed by the Soviets. Zorn's supposed mission was to explore ways the U.S. could keep the existing governments in power and prevent Central America from going communist and invading the U.S. across the Arizona border.

Treaties barred direct interference, and Zorn's mission was not what the White House claimed. Zorn's mission was to find covert ways for the U.S. to get arms, ammunition, tanks, trucks, aircraft, and money to the Central American governments. Also a flock of U.S. military officers to train troops. No one was to know—not Congress, the press, the voters, and not, as the writer of the article in Streeter's thick black book put it, "the court of world opinion." For a few months the secret operation went smoothly, paid for from a special White House fund Congress had no power to audit. Army pay rose sharply in El Salvador, Honduras, Los Inocentes, and hungry young men signed up. In hot sunlight, against a background of lush green mountains, they marched up and down in brand-new uniforms with brand-new M-16s on their shoulders, or crawled with them in the dust, while their drill instructors yelled at them in Iowa high school Spanish.

Then Zorn's paranoia got out of hand. To keep Soviet ships from bringing arms to the rebels of Los Inocentes, he ordered the harbor at Los Raderos mined. A Norwegian freighter loaded with lumber and canned sardines blew up and sank, and Zorn's mission came unraveled. Reporters flocked to Tegucigalpa, San Salvador, Los Raderos—Adam Streeter among them. Congress held hearings. On campuses across the country students marched and shouted against U.S. involvement in Central America. Congress revoked a new and legitimate aid bill. Red-faced State Department spokesmen spluttered into microphones. The scandal peaked and faded. The President's popularity rose. The goat was Lothrop Zorn, who after three days before a congressional subcommittee, simply faded out of sight. Dave's eyes dropped shut. He shook his head, blinked his eyes, took off the glasses, rubbed his eyes hard with his fingertips. He sat up, swung his feet to the floor, laid the book aside with the glasses on it, and tried the brandy again. He needed a cigarette, and he'd forgotten to bring the pack down from the loft. He tottered to his feet and went to the desk, to the bar. No cigarettes. He sighed and climbed the stairs. In the shadows of the loft, he groped for the pack and lighter on the small table next to the bed. The bed jounced. Cecil sat up.

"What's going on?"

"Everything's fine," Dave said. "I just couldn't sleep." He lit a cigarette. "I've been reading in that current events annual Streeter kept on his desk. Lying here tonight, I remembered reading a listing he'd marked—for one Colonel Lothrop Zorn, U.S. Marine Corps, retired. And I reread it."

"Mmm." Cecil flopped back down, pulled pale covers up over his dark shoulders. His voice came muffled by pillows. "And you got to wondering, could he be El Coronel?"

"That's what I got to wondering." Dave sat on his side of the bed. "What I read was suggestive." He blew away smoke. It drifted up into the skylight where leaf-strewn panes divided the star map into long rectangles. "Do you know anything about Zorn?"

"*Poquito,*" Cecil murmured. "I'll tell you in the morning."

At ten after six, the panes of the skylight showed blue sky. The telephone was ringing. Dave groaned, turned groggily, reached out for it. But it stopped ringing before his hand located it. He glanced over his shoulder. Cecil had left the bed. Dave didn't hear his voice from below. He must be in the cookshack or the front building, taking the call there. Dave looked at the bedside instrument again. A light winked beside the pushbuttons. He sighed, sat up, rubbed a hand down his face, and picked up the receiver. The voice at the other end of the line was Leppard's. "Brandstetter?" it said. "You were wrong. I did not see. Nobody came."

"Is Porfirio's sister all right?" Dave said.

"Stiff neck from sleeping in a chair," Leppard said. "Otherwise fine. I'm using her phone. She's fixing me breakfast."

"You're in for a treat." Dave shook a cigarette from the pack beside the phone, set it in his mouth, clicked a flame from the lighter, lit the cigarette, and coughed. "You calling somebody to replace you when you leave?"

"You really think it's necessary?" Leppard asked, then said *"Gracias"* to someone. "This is half a mango," he told Dave, surprised.

"I really think it's necessary," Dave said.

"Okay," Leppard said. "Till noon. But it's a waste of time. Much as I hate to crow, you guessed wrong."

"I hope so," Dave said. "But I doubt it."

"Did you sleep?" Leppard said. "You looked beat."

"I slept," Dave said. "Thanks. I appreciate it."

"Thank Frosty the Snowgirl," Leppard said.

When Dave stepped out of the shower, a mug of coffee waited for him on the surround of the washbasin, steaming in the steam that filled the room and fogged the mirror at which he shaved. He climbed the stairs naked, carrying the coffee mug, drank some coffee, lit a cigarette, took another swallow of coffee, wedged the cigarette in an ashtray, and dressed. Tan hopsack jeans, a gold velour pullover. He slid his feet into canvas shoes with rope soles, pushed cigarettes and lighter into a pocket, and carried the coffee mug back downstairs. The black book lay where he'd left it under the lamp, reading glasses beside it. He picked up the book and dropped it. It splayed open and a folded paper slid out. He set down the coffee mug, bent for book and paper, tucked the book under an arm, put on the reading glasses, unfolded and peered at the paper. It was a Xerox of the clipping he'd found at Underhill's the other morning—about the President offering five hundred thousand dollars reward for the capture of terrorists. He laid it back in the book, and carried book and coffee mug across the uneven patio bricks, ducking the lianas of a flowering vine, to the cookshack. The cookshack door was open and good smells came out. He worked the screen and stepped inside.

"Sorry the phone woke you." Cecil was at the stove. He wore white jeans and that was all. "I tried to stop it, but I couldn't jump that fast."

"Forget it." Dave kissed his naked shoulder and peered at what he was up to. "Buckwheat cakes, country sausage, and eggs over easy."

"And biscuits in the oven," Cecil said. "You better be hungry." He kissed Dave's mouth lightly, took the coffee mug from him, noticed the book. "We going to start Bible readings at breakfast?"

"This is my calorie counter," Dave said, and laid the book on the table. "I carry it with me everywhere."

"Lightning"—Cecil reached plates down from a cupboard and laid them on a counter—"is going to strike you, one of these days." Dave poured coffee into the mug Cecil had forgotten, and carried the mug to the table, where he set it at Cecil's place. He took his seat. Cecil shoveled griddle cakes, sausage, and eggs onto the plates, brought them to the table, set them down, and returned to the giant stove for the hot biscuits. Whistling and shaking his fingers, he dropped the biscuits one by one into a napkin-lined basket, brought the basket to the table, and sat himself down. "It's all hot. Don't burn yourself."

"You were going to tell me about Lothrop Zorn." Dave took a biscuit from the basket, broke it open, cut a chunk of butter to melt inside it. "The background I got from the book—but what happened after those congressional hearings? What became of him?"

Cecil burned his mouth on sausage, and hastily gulped orange juice. "He started a military training camp in some swamp in South Carolina."

"His own private army?" Dave took a bite of the biscuit. Perfect. He swallowed some coffee, and buttered his hotcakes. "The way they tell it down in San Feliz?"

"Only he was breaking all kinds of laws," Cecil said. "Our lawmakers don't permit training foreign troops on U.S. soil." Cecil handed Dave the brown pottery pitcher of maple syrup. "Zorn claimed he was only trying to help out our Central American allies by shaping up their field officers. See, after his debacle in Los Inocentes, Congress got strict about U.S. officers training armies down there. Made a law our people could not get out on the field to teach them. The army game then became to put the officers indoors with TV cameras and the men outdoors with TV receivers, but that was kind of awkward."

"Really?" Dave laughed and tried the buckwheat cakes. "I never heard that. That's funny."

"Nothing's funny to Zorn, nothing that gets in his way, fighting the communists." Cecil chewed sausage, reached for the syrup, drizzled it on the pancakes. "And South Carolina sympathized with him. Until one of his trainees died and his Salvadoran relatives raised hell about it. Then Carolina kicked Zorn out. Nothing else they could do." Cecil set down the syrup.

"How long ago was this?" Dave said.

Cecil shrugged. "Two years?" He ate with concentration for a few minutes. "You think he's down there in the San Macintosh—the mountains back of the produce ranches? You think he's El Coronel? For real?"

"Isn't that how it adds up to you?" Dave said. "What Tamayo saw—men in combat camouflage running along a dry creek bed, being shot at by others from the woods? With live ammunition? Doesn't that sound like Zorn?"

"It sounds like insanity." Cecil's look was troubled. "And you should forget it now. Leave it to Leppard."

"Leppard is looking in the wrong places."

"How are you going to find Zorn?" Cecil said. "Search those mountains on horseback?"

"He came down from the mountains," Dave said. "His men did. More than once. He's desperate."

"Not so desperate he sent them to kill Porfirio," Cecil said. "That didn't work."

Dave smiled thinly. "Then I'll have to think of something better, won't I?"

"I hope you don't," Cecil said. "I mean that. Adam Streeter is dead, Rafael, McGregor. You'll be next."

"He has to be stopped. I've got to find him. Somebody knows where he is." Dave ate thoughtfully for a minute. "Of course." He laid down his fork. "Duke Summers."

Cecil stared and swallowed hard. "You know Duke Summers?"

"He lives at the Grovers. We were old Army buddies."

"Jesus," Cecil said. A light, irregular tapping sounded on the patio bricks. He wiped his mouth with a napkin, pushed back his chair, rose, and went to the cookshack door. "Hello?" He pushed open the screen. "Can I help you?"

"Mr. Brandstetter?" The voice was Chrissie Streeter's.

Dave said, "Right here," and rose to go meet her. She wore a man's hat with a wide brim, a tweed jacket too large in the shoulders and too long, and trousers with twice the yardage required. It was the latest look. That slender white cane with the red tip wasn't all she carried. In her other hand was a white plastic bag from a department store, something black bulging out of it. "Let me take that," Dave said, and took it. "This is my associate, Cecil Harris. Christina Streeter."

"Chrissie," she said, and held out her thin, nail-bitten hand for Cecil to shake. "This is a strange place." She stood in the doorway. "You're eating breakfast."

"It's three buildings," Dave said. "This is the cookshack. The other two are for living and sleeping, respectively. Have you had breakfast?"

"Coffee and toast would be fine," she said. "I've found out something. Something terrible. I didn't want to call the police. I thought you'd know what to do."

Dave took her arm that seemed very thin inside the bulky coat sleeve, and led her inside and sat her at the table. "Would biscuits be all right? Fresh baked. Cecil is a dab hand with biscuits." He looked at Cecil, who seemed immobilized. He still stood at the door and was staring at Chrissie unblinking, with his mouth slightly ajar.

Chrissie nodded. "Biscuits sound lovely." She turned her face toward the door. "Cecil? You're very tall, aren't you?"

"No credit to me." Cecil shook himself out of his trance. "It just happened. I am also black." He went to a cupboard and brought down one of the handsome brown mugs and filled it with coffee for her. He found a small plate and brought this, with the coffee, to the table. The mug he set in front of her, the plate he took to his own place, where he buttered biscuits on it for her. "Twenty-five years old. I work in television news."

Dave sat on his chair, set the slick white bag on the floor, and pulled the contents out. It was a black wet suit with yellow and red leg and arm stripes. A long rip was in the left upper leg. As if the rubber had caught on something sharp. He laid the wet suit over the back of the empty fourth chair at the table, and saw that in the bag lay a face mask and black swim fins. He pulled these out, and beneath them metal gleamed. A pair of wire cutters. "Where did you find these?"

"In a locker in the cabana at Mother's," Chrissie said, and to Cecil, "these biscuits are heavenly."

"We've got honey, if you want," Cecil said, "orange marmalade, lime marmalade, currant jelly, raspberry jam—"

"I like them this way," she said, "just with butter."

"Whose are they?" Dave asked her.

"Do you want cream or sugar for your coffee?" Cecil said.

"Both, please," she said. "Two sugars. Ken Kastouros," she told Dave. "My mother's boyfriend. It was his locker. I wanted to swim, and I didn't have my cap. And I knew he had one—he has all this awful greasy hair, you know, and he likes to keep it that way. And so I jimmied his locker to get the cap, and here was all this weird stuff. Dan'l and I talk on the phone all the time. I can't talk to Mother except it turns into a fight. And Ken only wants to talk about sex. Anyway, Dan'l told me you thought somebody got in and killed Adam by coming by water, cutting the fence, and climbing over the roofs. And then I found these things. It took me a while to get away without them stopping me, but I thought you ought to know."

"How did you get here?"

"In a taxi. I had your card. I gave it to the driver." Cecil stood by her, leaned beside her to sugar and cream her coffee.

When the spoon stopped rattling, she said, "It's bad, isn't it? I mean, it must have been Ken. I knew she was sick. In her mind. With all that drinking and doping. And I knew she was furious at Gandy for not leaving her her money. She likes money. She has to have it. She only knows one way to live, and it costs a lot. But I never thought she'd kill Adam. I thought she still loved him. I thought all that hate talk was cover-up, you know?"

"You think she talked Kastouros into murder?"

Chrissie took a quick swallow of coffee and shook her head. "She must have promised him money. From Adam's insurance. He's like her about money. Because they're beautiful, they think they deserve to be rich. I guess some women have always been like that—it's a way to survive in a man's world. But Ken's no woman—and he's the very same way. He trades his looks for whatever he wants. That's what Adam said. And he was right." She munched biscuit for a thoughtful moment, butter oozing down her chin. She felt it, wiped at it with her fingers, licked her fingers, gave a bitter little laugh. "I wasn't there more than a few hours when Ken tried to get me to go to bed with him."

Cecil stared. "In your mother's house?"

She nodded. "I don't want to go back there."

"Stay here," Cecil said. "We've got a guest room. Brand-new. Never been used."

"He wasn't thinking, was he?" Chrissie said. "Good looks don't mean anything to me. I can't see them."

"I saw him," Dave said, "at the funeral."

"I didn't know you were there," Chrissie said.

"I came to locate Adam's lawyer—for a friend."

"And what do you think?" she said. "Is Ken beautiful?"

"It isn't going to help him with Sergeant Jeff Leppard of the LAPD," Dave said, and stretched a hand up to take down the receiver of the yellow phone.

Leppard yawned. It was late afternoon, and he was no longer sleek. His sweaty jacket hung on the back of his chair. His shirt had wilted. After the old manner of Ken Barker, he had unbuttoned the collar and pulled down the knot of his handsome tie. Rough beard stubble showed, and his eyes were bloodshot. In front of him on his desk lay stained orange paper wrappings from taquitos he'd had brought in from an Olvera Street stand. A Styrofoam cup held the dregs of coffee. Not a crumb was on the papers, and Leppard crushed them now and dropped them into his wastebasket. He finished off the cold coffee, made a face, dropped the cup after the wrappers, and belched. Sourly.

"There's Mexican food," he said, "and Mexican food."

"You're thinking of Porfirio's sister's kitchen."

"Wish I was there." Leppard sighed and changed the subject: "He ripped the wet suit leg on the cut fence."

"Which was already cut when he got there?" Dave said.

"Way he tells it. He crawled through, and after that he doesn't remember anything. Somebody knocked him on the head. Doctor confirmed that. A hard bang."

"But not so hard it broke the skin or gave him a concussion," Dave said. "Not so hard that when he came to and didn't see anyone, he didn't follow orders and go right on to Streeter's door, let himself in with Brenda Streeter's key, sneak up those spiral stairs, and find Adam Streeter dead on the floor of his workroom with a gun in his hand."

"It was four in the morning," Leppard said.

"And you've located a witness who saw Brenda Streeter parked in the red Seville in the dark on the far side of the water?" Dave lit a cigarette. "Waiting for him?"

"A surfer kid," Leppard said, "impatient for morning. He saw Kastouros come out of the water. Told us about the rip in the wet suit. She handed him a beach towel to wrap himself in before he got into the car."

"And Brenda says—?" Dave asked.

"Nothing. She's got a lawyer. Albright."

"The one with the funny voice?" Dave said.

"Dead-sounding—yeah."

"But he represented Adam Streeter in the divorce. He despises her. Why would she choose him?"

Leppard shrugged, smiled faintly. "He won, didn't he?"

"Right." Dave sighed and stood up. "So, is the District Attorney interested?"

"Fascinated." Leppard yawned again. "Jesus, I'm tired."

"Is he going to let Underhill go? And Hunsinger, and Fleur? Everybody can't be guilty."

Leppard laughed briefly, shook his head, pushed heavily to his feet. "You're right, and I think he's feeling— what word do I want?" Leppard scratched his head, delicately again, with a little finger, just above the white stripe in his hair. "Bewildered?" The ghost of a chuckle came and went. "I wouldn't advise you to bring up your midnight commandos to him right now. We might have to drag him off kicking and screaming."

"I don't know where they fit," Dave said.

"They're a sidebar." Leppard took his jacket off the back of his chair and shrugged into it. "I told you what it had to be—simple murder for money. Better than that—a family affair." He touched Dave's shoulder and moved past him to open his office door. The busy noises of the detective squad room flooded in. "Alcoholic wife, opportunistic boyfriend, overinsured husband. The old, old story." He left the room. "Neat."

Dave followed him. "Too neat. If the commandos didn't kill Streeter, they sure as hell killed his contact, Rafael."

"Hunsinger lied to you," Leppard said, "why not Porfirio?"

"For what reason? Look, think about the timing. Why should Brenda have picked that particular night to send Kastouros to kill her ex-husband? The night when he'd given Mike Underhill the cash to buy that plane? The night of the day when Adam Streeter had driven off to get the final facts he needed to break the hottest story of the decade? Why not the night before, or the night after?"

"Coincidence." Leppard pushed out into a corridor and made for the elevators, Dave following him. Leppard said, "I don't know." He pressed a button to summon an elevator. "Only two things do I know at this moment." He read his watch. "I haven't slept for a day and a night and I need to do that." An electronic ping sounded. A red, down-pointing arrow lit up above the elevator doors. "And you will figure it out all by yourself." The elevator doors slid open. Two plainclothes officers stepped out. Leppard and Dave stepped in. Leppard asked, "You've got the girl at your house? Pretty. Shame she's blind."

"It's a shame somebody killed her father," Dave said. The elevator doors closed. The elevator started down.

"If the mother is indicted, and she's the guardian—"

"It's temporary," Dave said. "By default. Only living relative. She lost custody at the time of the divorce—you know that. She's a drunk and a chemical dependent."

"The County will want custody of the girl," Leppard said.

"I'm more interested in what she wants," Dave said. "She loved her father. She's bearing up, so far. But I think there's a limit to how much more she can take. She hasn't done anything to deserve being in anybody's custody."

"I'll speak to the DA," Leppard said. The elevator eased to a stop. The doors opened. "Tomorrow."

Cecil's flame-painted van was not in its place on the bricks of the brush-shadowed yard between the road and the front building. Dave slid the Jaguar into place, switched off its engine, frowned at his watch. Had he forgotten the day of the week? Were they supposed to meet at Romano's for dinner? He didn't think so. He opened the car door, stepped out, drew a deep breath, and moved his shoulders to ease their tenseness—he'd fought miles of heavy traffic from downtown. The car door fell closed with heavy gentleness. He locked it, and moved through the gathering dusk around the end of the front building. Grumpy. They'd kept Cecil working late again.

Then he remembered Chrissie. She'd be here, anyway. He smiled, sorted a key from other keys in the packet, and turned the lock in the front door, a broad door of thick glass panes clinched in wood. It swung inward, he stepped in, but big as the room was, he knew before his eyes could search the shadows that no one was here. He pulled the door shut, glanced for lights at the cookshack. No lights, but Chrissie didn't need lights, did she? She lived in the dark. He put his head in at the cookshack door. Again no one. He pulled this door shut and crossed under the trailing vine to unlock and open the door of the rear building. He stepped inside and didn't see her.

"Chrissie?" His voice went up to the loft where she might be—the new room. But she didn't answer, didn't show herself. He lightly rapped the bathroom door. No response. He opened it a crack. Empty. He called into the high raftered silence of the place once more. "Chrissie?" She wasn't here. Cecil must have taken her with him to his workplace at Channel Three. The room had stored up heat from the sun on its shake roof all day. It smelled of pine sap and, underlying that, the faint recollection of horse, from the days when it was a stable. He opened windows, outside which untrimmed branches crowded. He let the door stand open, shed the light windbreaker he'd worn, went to the bar, and put together a pitcher of martinis.

He poured one over ice into a deep glass, stowed the pitcher in the small refrigerator back of the bar, and took drink and cigarettes out onto the patio. A broad bench of redwood planks surrounded the trunk of the oak. He set on the bricks three potted plants to make a place for himself, brushed away with a hand dried leaves and fern fronds, sat down, leaned back against the tree trunk with a sigh, and tasted the martini. He lit a cigarette, watched a light breeze take the smoke, and gazed up through the gnarled branches of the oak where the sky was changing colors from blue to green, from pink to flame, from lavender to smoky purple. Before he had finished the martini, the sky was black, and stars showed. He went to the rear building, switched on the lamps there, poured another drink for himself, then crossed to the cookshack.

He thought about London in 1945, the only time he'd been there, how long the days held on in summer, until almost ten at night. Of course, that winter with Duke Summers in Berlin, night had come at three in the afternoon when snow was threatening. And morning had been morning only according to clocks and watches. Pitch dark, and bone cold. He sliced mushrooms at the sink, melted butter in a small pan to sauté them, heated the grill to make an omelette in which to fold the mushrooms. He tore up crisp lettuce, chopped a tomato, poured oil and vinegar over these on a small plate. Sliced chunks of French bread from a long loaf. Set the table. He had just begun to eat when the phone rang.

"Mr. Brandstetter, Trinket's out."

"Dan'l?" Dave said. "What do you mean?"

"The Gernsbachs' cat. I knew Mr. De Lis would never let her get away from him. It had to be Harry. He's the one she can always trick."

"You mean the Gernsbachs have come home?"

"Their boat's back. I thought you'd want to know."

Dave's heart thumped. "Have you seen them, talked to them?"

"I tried to return Trinket," Dan'l said. "I went around and rang their doorbell, but nobody came. I didn't see any lights. But if Trinket's out, they're there."

"Don't try again," Dave said. "Let me handle it."

"You coming?" Dan'l sounded excited.

"Right away. Twenty minutes at the longest. Sit tight."

"Ouch," Dan'l said. "Trinket, damn it, that hurts."

Dan'l waited for him at the gates. Clara in her starchy uniform, her bulldog jaw set, her bright green knitting needles clicking ferociously, only glanced with her grandmotherly gray eyes at Dave, a look of disapproval, but she worked the switch to set the gates parting, and Dave with cheery thanks drove through. Dan'l got into the Jaguar. He didn't have Trinket with him.

"She's locked in our bathroom," Dan'l said. "Last time I found her out and put her in there she had toilet paper all over. The whole roll unrolled. Kleenex torn out of the box. All the medicine chest stuff out, piled in the sink, towels on the floor. She's a demon."

Dave parked the Jaguar and they both got out. The night breeze rustled the dark water beyond the ground lights of the place. On the far side, the lights of other condominium windows wavered yellow in the water. The boats rocked at their moorings, the metal clips on ropes clinking against the metal of masts. Dave followed Dan'l along narrow outdoor passages to the Gernsbach place. Dan'l's Nikes made no sound, nor did Dave's plimsolls. He put a hand on Dan'l's bony chest to stop the boy in shadow away from the door. He stepped up to the door, put his ear to it, and listened. All was quiet. He used a slip of metal from his wallet to work the lock. It opened as easily for him as had the Streeter lock the other night. The door swung softly inward. Dave raised a cautioning hand to Dan'l, who was a pale thin shape among shadowy shrubs, slipped inside the Gernsbach place, and soundlessly closed the door behind him.

The layout was a mirror image of the Streeter place. Here, too, light came in through French doors from the swimming-pool patio. Its wavering glow showed Dave French provincial furniture and eighteenth-century carpets. But the spiral staircase was the same. He went and stood at its foot, looking up into darkness, straining to hear. Maybe he imagined it, but it seemed to him faint sounds came from up there—soft electronic beeps and clicks. He slipped off the plimsolls, left them, and cautiously climbed the stairs. On the first gallery level he paused, looking for light at the edge of doors. Nothing. But the sounds were clearer here, and he went up on to the third level, and there light thin as a knife blade shone under a door. He opened the door.

A big, fiftyish man in rumpled denim pants and jacket, a captain's cap pushed back on thinning crinkly gray hair, sat at a computer. Except around the eyes, his face was deeply, painfully sunburned. So were the big hands that flew up from the keyboard in surprise and fright. He stood up, and the small typist's chair he'd sat in wheeled backward and fell over. The man held his hands up as if Dave had a gun trained on him. The hands trembled. The man's eyes bulged.

"Who are you? Are you one of them? I swear I saw—"

"I'm Dave Brandstetter. And you're Harry Gernsbach, yes?"

"You are trespassing." There was the ghost of an accent. Germany, that concentration camp, were long ago. "Get out."

Dave showed him a business card, but Gernsbach only goggled at it. Dave said, "I'm a death-claims investigator for insurance companies. I'm looking into the death of your neighbor, Adam Streeter. I've been waiting for you to come home, so I could ask you—"

"That's all settled," Gernsbach said. "Mike Underhill murdered him. It has been on television, time and again."

"But it's not true, is it?" Dave said. "If it was Mike Underhill you saw kill Adam Streeter, you'd have phoned the police. You wouldn't have run away to sea without telling anybody. You wouldn't have stayed in hiding for days."

"Hiding? Hiding?" Gernsbach tried bluster, but not ably. "I have been sailing. Fishing. With my wife."

"What brought you back?" Dave said.

"It is only temporary. Month-end business." He made a half gesture at the computer. "I am a savings and loan director. It was necessary to review certain accounts." He broke off. "How did you know I was here?"

"You let the cat out," Dave said, "when you came in. A neighbor saw her, and gave me a phone call."

"*Scheisse!*" Gernsbach picked the chair up and slammed it down on its casters. He stuck out a white-bristled chin at Dave. "I can tell you nothing. Go now. I must work. Then we go to sea again. A long cruise. To the South Pacific."

"Uh-huh. They saw you, didn't they?" Dave said. "That figured. It was the only explanation. The curtains were open in your bedroom, you woke up, and saw them across the way—men in combat gear, crossing the roof, swing down on a rope to the balcony of Streeter's workroom. You got up and went to the French doors to see better, right? And you saw them shoot him, heard the gun. And before you could duck out of sight, they saw you. That's why you ran away, and why you're going away again, for a long time, until Mike Underhill is convicted of that murder—and the real killers know they're safe."

"Streeter courted danger," Gernsbach said. "He should not have been living here among quiet people. He hungered for violence." Gernsbach snorted. "What did he know? Had he lived under the Nazis? So—he brought it here. Terrorism." He found a bottle and glasses in a file cabinet. He rattled them and pushed a long amber drink at Dave with a shaky hand. "In Marina del Rey." He wagged his head and drank deeply. "The world is turning ugly again.

As in Hitler's time." He eyed Dave bleakly. "Who are they? Where do they come from?"

"I'm not sure." Dave tried the drink—Wild Turkey. "It had to do with a story on Los Inocentes he was writing."

Gernsbach snorted. "This government can't keep out of there, and neither could Adam. I warned him. "Political fanatics are all alike; you will end up dead. Then what will become of Chrissie?" He only grinned at me."

"You should have phoned the police," Dave said.

"I would have been a corpse by the time they got here," Gernsbach said. "Terrorists do not let witnesses live."

"How many were there?" Dave said.

"Three. Young, from the way they moved. Strange. They were dressed for combat, but I saw no guns."

"Streeter came up with the gun," Dave said, "which was bad judgment." He drank off the whiskey and set the glass on the desk. "Call the police now—Jeff Leppard, homicide. You don't want Mike Underhill to sit on death row for this."

"It cannot be helped," Gernsbach said. "If I show my face, those storm troopers will kill me."

He swung the Jaguar in at an almost empty parking lot beside a white clapboard restaurant with a spouting black whale painted on its side. He got out of the car to take down the gritty receiver of a pay phone in a half booth with sea-fogged glass side panels. He rang his house. No one answered. He rang the television station. Cecil had not been in today. He'd said he was going out of town. Dave scowled at that and hung up. He moved away from the phone, turned back, and punched the number of the east side house.

The sister who cooked so well answered. Had she heard from Porfirio? She answered in Spanish, with tears in her voice, "He has disappeared. She went out to the market, and when she returned he was gone. The neighbors said two men came, in cowboy boots and straw hats, and took him away."

"In a four-wheel-drive vehicle?" Dave said.

"*Sí.* On big tires. With black glass at the windows. They will kill him, now—no?"

"Maybe not," Dave said, cold in his belly.

"I have been to the church and have lighted a candle for him," she said. "One also for you, *señor.*"

"*Gracias,*" he said.

But he would need more help than that. He punched four-one-one, and asked for the number.

## 15

FORTY-ODD YEARS ago he had crammed German at an army language school in downtown LA. The hours were long. He always left late. The streets were empty at night then. It had felt eerie—that lonely half-mile walk he'd made each midnight to the trolley barn to catch an almost empty big red car to his barracks in South Pasadena. The walk had taken him through the district called Little Tokyo. But the Japanese had all been rounded up and shipped off to internment camps. The shops that had sold fabrics and vases and beautiful cabbages were vacant. Off the boards that blanked their windows, his steps had echoed block after deserted block, loud and strange to his own ears. He hadn't felt afraid. Who was there to be afraid of? He had felt that he was alone on earth. He felt that way now. Tall glass buildings glowed that hadn't been here forty-odd years ago. A remote roar of traffic reached him from the freeways that met, knotted, and untangled themselves here at the city's heart. But no automobiles drove these streets. He saw no human beings. LA was a city of the dead at night.

The Grovers was stepped terraces outside, and inside was fumed oak, deep-buttoned leather, thick old mirrors. The light from crystal chandeliers was subdued. The carpets on marble floors and staircases were old, thick, handsome. Palms grew large in brass pots in corners. All sound was muted, the whisper of shuffling cards, the click of billiard balls, the rustle of *Wall Street Journal* pages in the hands of readers in wing chairs, even the rare laughter from the throats of judges, corporate lawyers, millionaire brokers, top management executives, retired generals, celebrated surgeons, overpaid officials and bureaucrats from City Hall, County Courthouse, Federal Building. And from Sacramento—the governor was a member of the Grovers.

Carl Brandstetter had joined in the late 1920s, when Medallion, his life insurance company, had rocketed to success. In 1947, when Dave came back from Europe to join the company, his father had put in his name for membership. He was accepted, but he had scarcely set foot in the place since. A lunch now and then with his father had been the sum of it. Money and power were all they talked about, thought about, cared about here. Not Dave's subjects. Not then. Not now. Now he was here to call in a marker.

The bar hadn't changed—dark paneling, dark leathers, a brass foot rail polished to a high sheen. Very old black men tended the long bar. These old men wore white jackets, just as always in the past. How many hundred such jackets had they worn out in their long lifetimes here? He read his watch and hiked himself onto a stool, and one of the old men came creakily to serve him. He had better go on with American whiskey. But not Wild Turkey—the proof was too high. He wanted his wits. It was a very old marker. And he had to drive home afterward. He asked for Jack Daniel's Black.

The bartender peered at him with eyes whose whites were the dulled hue of very old porcelain. "It would be Mr. Brandstetter, is that right? Been a long time since we seen you here, sir."

"You're thinking of my father," Dave said. "He's no longer living."

"Oh." The creases in the black face deepened. "I'm sorry to hear that. Then you'd be—let me see can I remember—David?"

Dave smiled. "You have a wonderful memory."

"So they tell me," the bartender said, "but you look a good deal like your father. He was a fine man." The bartender moved away, and with the studied motions of the very old chose a short sturdy glass of cut Waterford. He dropped ice into this. Then with respect for painful joints and a brittle spine he stooped to lift the square whiskey bottle from its place on a softly lighted glass shelf. He measured whiskey into the glass not with a jigger but by practiced eye. The small paper napkin he laid on the bar was imprinted with the black silhouette of an orange tree that was the emblem of the Grovers and, with all deliberate speed, he set the glass down on the napkin in front of Dave. "Your father was a Scotch drinker," he said.

"Johnnie Walker," Dave said. "Rough and tough."

"I don't drink myself," the bartender said, "never did. But I guess each brand is a little different, ain't it?"

"Very different." Dave lifted his glass. "Thank you."

"Nice to have you here." The old man gave a little bow of his darkly polished bald head with its fringe of white hair, and moved rheumatically away.

It was past dinnertime. Behind him round tables drowsed in candlelight under snowy, heavy linen cloths. In a farther room men played cards at game tables, or sat talking in groups, or reading. In a room farther off still, men bent over billiard tables. Cigar smoke tinged the air. Dave smiled to himself. The aroma was unmistakable—Havana. The members of the Grovers might hate Dr. Castro and all his works, but there was a limit to self-sacrifice. Dave snubbed out his cigarette in a small glass ashtray with the Grovers orange tree stenciled on its bottom, and checked his watch again. He lit another cigarette and slowly finished off the Jack Daniel's. A light hand touched his shoulder.

"Mr. Brandstetter." The speaker was a trim young man with a haircut so neat it looked painted on. His clothes were neat, new, and fitted him, but he stood stiffly in them. His face was stiff. His eyes, of no special color, held no special expression, either. He might have been a store-window dummy, except that when Dave nodded he spoke again, politely, but without expression. "Director Summers will see you now. If you'll come with me, please?" Dave left his cigarette, got off the stool, and followed him past the grand staircase to the elevators. He read his watch again, and smiled. It was precisely ten thirty.

In the elevator—a cage of wrought-iron tracery with a worn brass plate for the worn brass floor buttons, it shuddered upward on ancient cables that flapped in the hollow shaft—Dave thought about Duke Summers. He had read about him now and then in newspapers and magazines, but decades had passed since he'd seen or spoken to him. Would he recognize him now? The young Army attorney Dave remembered was willowy, pretty, rather than handsome, and frightened by an effeminacy as natural to him as breathing. Duke had planned a career that was not going to allow for that.

While they had roomed together, served together in intelligence after the war in Germany, Dave had tried to school him out of his girlish mannerisms. But Duke had compulsions he couldn't control—to paint his face, to dress in women's clothes—which he concealed from Dave as from everyone else. Until a night of sleet and rain when Dave had to rescue him from a blue-eyed, blond, blackmailing teenage boy in a Darmstadt alley. Which ought to have taught Duke a lesson—it was a near thing; the MPs almost caught them. It didn't teach him a lesson. It took a far closer call, a few months later, to do that.

The elevator jerked to an uncertain halt, the young man clattered open the grille gate, pushed the door beyond it, and led Dave down a quiet corridor between fumed oak doors with small brass nameplates. The door he opened for Dave led into a large handsome sitting room. From a good-looking armchair an old man rose, red-faced, jowly, with a white moustache, white eyebrows, a paunch. He wore gray flannel trousers, a dark blue blazer with brass buttons, a raw silk shirt, a silk scarf knotted at the throat, and he came forward with his hand out and a smile of fine dentures.

"Dave!" He roared a laugh whose masculinity would have shamed John Wayne, seized Dave's hand in a crushing grip, and pumped it hard. "Dave, I can't believe it." He wrapped Dave in a bear hug, chortling. He stood Dave at arm's length, gripping his shoulders. "My God, how long has it been?" None of this surprised Dave. Right out of the Army, Duke had married, and within six years had produced five sturdy children, and had gone on to shape a career even more remarkable than the one he had dreamed of back in Germany. What disturbed Dave was the film of sweat on the great man's forehead, and how his eyes in their pouches darted this way and that, never settling on him. "Sit down, man, sit down. This is my aide, Bob Shales." Summers flapped a hand toward a chair and Dave took it. A handshake with Shales didn't seem indicated. "What will you drink? This calls for a drink, right?"

"Jack Daniel's," Dave said to Shales, "thank you."

Summers swept up a glass of half-melted ice cubes from the table by his chair, handed it to Shales, and settled back as the young man soundlessly left the room. "You look great," Summers said to Dave. "Done well for yourself, right? Big insurance mogul, isn't that it? Richest corporations in America. You always did have the smarts."

"I was a department head," Dave said, "death-claims investigations. Now I'm a private investigator—same line. It was my father who was the mogul, Duke."

"You look as if you're doing all right." The restless unhappy eyes sized up Dave's clothes. "You arrived in a Jaguar. You buy your clothes at Brooks Brothers. Those are handmade shoes. Your home in Laurel Canyon assesses at a million two hundred thou."

"You've been checking up," Dave said. "The house is just a couple of old stables updated. Don't put too much stock in real estate prices these days."

"All right. You're a poverty case. But your bank account says otherwise. Your portfolios."

"Why did you check up on me, Duke?"

"It's been forty years. People change. It's called screening. A routine procedure." He waved a hand and practiced his avuncular smile. "Don't feel bad. All kinds of people want me dead. My staff worries about that. I'm like a goddam art masterpiece or something. One that nobody gets to see."

"I'm honored," Dave said.

Summers made a sour face. "It gets old sometimes. Especially for the family, you know? Wife and kids. There isn't a photograph of them in existence, did you know that? They can't even live in this country. We don't use the mails. Everything goes by diplomatic courier. Christmas cards, anniversary presents, everything."

"You wanted to be a great man," Dave said.

"The young make a lot of mistakes," Summers grunted.

"Lonely at the top?" Dave said.

Shales came in with very large, squat glasses of ice and whiskey, held the tray for Dave to take his, set Summers's down under the lamp beside his chair. "Anything else?" he said. And Summers gave him a very different sort of smile—not the public one he'd given Dave, but a private one, full of affection. "That's all, Bobby, thanks. Good night."

"Good night, Duke," Shales said, with a new humanity in his own expression, a note of tenderness in his voice. "Mr. Brandstetter? Nice to have met you."

"Yes," Dave said, "good night." And to Summers, when Shales had gone out and shut the door behind him, "Not so lonely at the top?"

"You know me so well." Summers laughed, and picked up his glass and held it high. "To old times," he said, and drank. "You look young, Dave. I never get time to keep in trim." He studied Dave. "I don't believe you've gained a pound since Berlin."

"Lost a little," Dave said, and tasted his whiskey. "I never get time to gain."

The big manly laugh burst out again. "I often think—do you remember the night we liberated that *Bierhalle* in the basement on Kreutzer Strasse, and the fat woman—"

"I remember breaking into the headquarters of the military police and stealing from the files the record of your arrest in that transvestite bar, so they couldn't drum you out of the service in disgrace. Do you remember that?"

Some of the claret flush drained from Summers's bloated face. All the light of laughter left his eyes. The sweat shone on his forehead again. "Oh," he said. "I see."

"Do you remember that?" Dave said again.

Summers worked his mouth a moment without sound. Then he breathed in deeply through his nose and said crossly, "Yes, yes, of course I remember that. I've tried to forget it, but life isn't that long. What about it?"

"I did it because you were my friend and you needed help. And you were too shattered to do it yourself. You'd given up. Sat there on your cot shivering, drinking. You were done for."

Summers sulked. "You took an awful chance."

"Someone had to," Dave said. "It's why you're here."

Summers peered at him sideways. "You want me to thank you?"

Dave grinned. "You cried on my shoulder in gratitude."

"I was weepy in those days," Summers grunted. "A regular girl. What do you want, Dave?"

"Find Colonel Lothrop Zorn, U.S. Marine Corps, retired," Dave said, "and lock him up."

"Good God." Summers half rose out of his chair. "What have you got to do with Lothrop Zorn?"

Dave told him the whole story.

"Fantastic." Summers waved a hand. "Forget it."

"Three murders?" Dave said. "Maybe four. Streeter—"

"A pain in the ass if ever one lived," Summers said.

"And the Inocentes boy, and McGregor, and now Porfirio?" Summers studied him. "And you're next—right?"

"They'll get my name out of Porfirio," Dave said.

"Come on. You're not afraid. You were never afraid of anything in your life. You're up to something. Politics?"

"No way. I never asked you for anything before," Dave said. "You owe me, Duke. I'm asking now."

Summers pulled down the corners of his mouth and shook his head. "You give me credit for power I haven't got."

"You can do whatever you want," Dave said. "The CIA takes all the flack, and nobody ever hears of your operation. Congress doesn't sweat you in front of committees. They don't question your budget. You haven't got one. Your money leaks from other agencies. Don't tell me you haven't got the power."

"I haven't got an army, Dave," Summers said. "Zorn has an army. Near San Gregornio. We know all about him."

"That he's murdering civilians?" Dave said.

"I don't know that now. That's your surmise."

"Check it out," Dave said, "arrest him, question him."

"The White House wouldn't like it. He's doing what they'd love to do, if only Congress would authorize it—training crack Inocentes troops and getting them down there to drive out the commies."

"Who's funding him?" Dave said. "You?"

Summers shook his head. "Private money. Old California cronies. But they've cooled off. They can't see any future in it. Zorn is hurting for money."

"Then why can't you move on him?"

"Because he's still a fair-haired boy." Summers raised a hand, palm outward, his smile crooked. "And don't threaten to expose my dress-up days in Germany, Dave. You won't do that. You're too decent. It's your fatal flaw."

"Don't trouble Bobby." Dave set down his drink and stood. "I can find my own way out."

## 16

IT WAS NEAR midnight. He was tired and disgusted, and he drove past the point where narrow, crooked Horseshoe Canyon Trail spurred up off Sagebrush Road. Why was it so dark? He braked the Jaguar, reversed, rolled backward to the crossroads, and understood why he had missed it. Light was supposed to shine down here through the trees. The light was out. He put his hand on the shift lever but didn't move it to drive. He sat frowning. The night was very still. It seemed to him he could hear his heart beat. *Thud* would be the exact word.

He probed the glove box, found a flashlight, lowered the window, put his head out, shone the light upward. The light fixture was at the end of a long armature that stretched from a splintery power pole. The glass that shielded the bulb was smashed. He set the gears to park, pulled the handbrake, and got out. Broken glass glinted at his feet. He heard a sound and beamed his light up the road. It showed him Hilda Vosper and her raggedy dog. She stopped and winced in the light. She fumbled for a flashlight in the pocket of her windbreaker and shone it on him.

"Oh, Mr. Brandstetter." She smiled and came on, the dog tugging at its leash. "Something's happened to the streetlight. I noticed it earlier. That's why I brought this."

"Some kid with a rock," Dave said.

Hilda Vosper tugged the dog back from the broken glass on the pavement—aged blacktop, gray, cracked, potholed. "Careful, sweetheart." The beam of her light and the beam of Dave's were enough for him to see the bright blue of her eyes. "Not a rock," she said, "a gun. I heard a shot—oh, when? About two hours ago. Told myself it was a backfire. You know how those monster trucks labor up the main road."

"I know," Dave said. He shone his light upward again, but it wasn't a strong light, and the leafage of the trees threw shadows that wouldn't let him see if there was a bullet hole in the metal hood of the lamp. "I'll settle for the rock," he said, "and the backfire. I'll call Water and Power in the morning."

"They have a night number," she said. "And a good thing, too. There's little enough street lighting up here as it is. I phoned them. There's a truck parked up above my place, but no sign of a repairman. They move in mysterious ways." With a little laugh and a lift of her hand, she padded in her tennis shoes on down Sagebrush Road, the flashlight beam swinging ahead of her, the dog darting in and out of it. "Good night." Her voice drifted back, musical and brave.

"Good night." Dave got wearily into the Jaguar and drove it a hundred yards up the trail to the sharp drop on the right, down into his brick-paved yard. The many small panes of the row of French doors that walled the front building gave back crooked reflections of the Jaguar's headlights. No sign of Cecil's van. Dave scowled. It had been eighteen hours. Where the hell was he? *Out of town.* What did that mean? It wasn't like him not to leave a note. Was Chrissie with him? He hoped so. He didn't like to think of her out on her own. No, they were together. Had to be.

He stepped out of the car, closed the door, locked it. It was dark as the bottom of a pocket here. In his rush to get to Harry Gernsbach, he'd forgotten to switch on the yard lights. It was all right. He knew his way. He blew out a long breath, trudged around the end of the front building and crossed the bumpy courtyard in the massive shadow of the oak. He wanted the rear building. That was where the bed was. And he was ready to drop. He fitted the key into the door and turned the key. Shoes scraped the bricks behind him. He half turned. And something struck him hard on the back of the skull.

He had a bad headache, the worst he could remember. His hands were tied. So were his ankles. Web belts bit in. That his hands were behind him made the way he sat awkward and cramping. Unconscious, he had settled at an angle, head resting against the window glass. The vehicle smelled of newness. The gloss of the fake leather seat felt new. They were traveling fast on a paved road but the suspension was stiff. His skull vibrated against the glass. He figured it would hurt less if that stopped, and he straightened on the seat.

The man next to him stirred but didn't waken. He wore an open-weave straw hat with the brim crimped the way they favored south of the border. He was the bigger of the two men Dave had glimpsed on that sunset street corner down the block from Porfirio's sister's house in Boyle Heights. The men he'd been afraid might get on board the bus with Porfirio. The men who had come for Porfirio in this Bronco, Blazer, Cherokee on its high tires at his other sister's house in Guadalupe. The man's chin was on his chest. He was dark, and had a hatchet profile. In the dim glow that reached back here from the dashboard, his loose lower lip glistened. He snored. If he had a gun, Dave couldn't see it.

Two men sat in the front seat—the thick-necked driver with a straw hat identical to this man's, and a passenger slouched down so Dave could see only his dirty gray hair. Porfirio. Not murdered. Not yet. *I have been to the church and lighted a candle for him.* Dave smiled bleakly to himself.

*And for you, also, señor.* He hoped they were long-burning candles. He looked out at empty fields and hills, black under a black, star-strewn sky. The road went straight, and the headlights reached out, following the road. He glanced at the rearview mirror. And met the driver's eyes. They were like agates, shiny and cold.

"You are awake," the driver said in Spanish. "Your head must be giving you pain. I regret that. If you can swallow them without water, I can give you aspirin tablets."

"I prefer whiskey to water," Dave said. "I will wait for some of El Coronel's whiskey. Is Porfirio all right?"

"We gave him something to make him sleep."

"And your partner, here?" The man's chin joggled on his chest with the movement of the car. The hat slowly slipped down over his eyes. He still snored.

"He is simply tired. He has driven hundreds of miles in the last two days. First to Los Angeles, then to Guadalupe, then back to Los Angeles. For you."

"He needn't have bothered," Dave said. The man laughed. "It was no trouble, *señor.*"

"What took you so long to get to me?" Dave said.

"Your name. Sheriff Dobbs in San Feliz had your name wrong. He called you Bannerman. But there is no insurance investigator of that name."

"But Porfirio had the name right?" Dave said.

"It is a difficult name," the driver said, "but, *sí,* he had it right. It was then simple to locate your house. I regret that it was necessary to hit you."

"It beats being shot," Dave said.

"We are not assassins," the man said. "Life is precious."

"Mine, but not Adam Streeter's?" Dave said.

"He made a foolish mistake." The driver lit a cigarette. The smell of the smoke was sweet. A Mexican cigarette. It took Dave back to trips he'd made as a kid with his father to Baja. A brown, dry, sunstruck land, empty, silent. The driver said, "He took a pistol from a drawer and tried to kill us. We were not even armed. We had only come to take him as we took you. His death was an accident. Regrettable."

"All right," Dave said, "but what about Rafael? He was executed. What did you think you were doing in the middle of the night—playing commandos? Disgusting. You are trigger-happy. Shooting out that streetlamp tonight. Are you children? You have a gun, you have to shoot it?"

"Do not make me angry," the driver said. "That is foolish. You are at my mercy. For your own sake, be quiet."

"It might have warned me you were waiting," Dave said. "A neighbor met me and said this truck was parked up the road. She thought it was a repair truck from the city. But if I hadn't been so tired, I might have gone to look at it, and I would have known whose truck it was. You were stupid."

"Not so stupid as you," the driver said. "You were not warned by the broken light. You did not go look at this truck. You are my prisoner. So which of us is stupid?"

"I was like your partner," Dave said. "All I could think of was sleep."

"Then sleep now," the driver said. "I am weary of the sound of your voice. And we still have a long way to travel."

"Rafael was one of you, wasn't he?" Dave said. "A soldier from Los Inocentes, training under El Coronel to return and spearhead the overthrow of the new government, and restore Cortez-Ortiz to power. You are all *chuchos*—little dogs."

"Rafael was a spy and a traitor," the driver said. "If you will not sleep of your own accord, *señor*, I will waken my partner, and we will give you the same kind of shot that we gave Porfirio, and make you sleep."

"Your war is your business," Dave said, "but not when you do your killing in this country. What you did was plain murder, three times over—to Rafael, to Adam Streeter, and to the pilot, McGregor. For this you will go to prison. I mean to see to that."

The driver gave a noisy sigh, leaned forward, jabbed out his cigarette, and rolled the truck to a long, slow halt on the shoulder of the road, the big tires crunching gravel and crackling dry brush. He switched the engine off, and a great silence wrapped them. He switched the headlights off, and by the dash light rummaged in the glove compartment. "Hector," he said, "wake up."

The man beside Dave snorted, jerked straight, pushed his hat back, blinked. *"Qué pasa?"* he said.

Gray morning light struggled in through a grimy window. He lay and blinked at the window for a while. His mind was numb. At last, he thought of his watch. It wasn't on his wrist. The wrist showed dark marks, and when he touched these, they stung. The other wrist was the same. He frowned, remembered, sat up sharply, and was sorry. He felt dizzy, and nausea surged in his throat. He closed his eyes, took deep rapid breaths, and the nausea went away. He cautiously opened his eyes again. The bed he lay on was a steel-pipe cot with clean sheets and blankets. The room was small. The plaster on the white walls was rough, and grime had lodged in it. Hammocks of dark cobweb hung in ceiling corners. A chair stood beside the bed, his shirt, jacket, tie hung over the back, his trousers across the straw seat, his watch, wallet, keys, cigarettes, lighter inside the coil of his belt on the trousers. He shifted, squinted at the floor. His shoes stood there, socks tucked into them.

The floorboards felt dusty, gritty when he walked to the window. The window frame had lost most of its paint. More paint flaked off when he worked the latch. He had to hammer the frame with the side of a fist to open the window. The hinges were rusty, stubborn, squeaky. Cold morning air came against his face. It smelled of pine. Old ponderosas grew up mountain slopes on all hands. They stood close to each other, big as they were, and showed no green, not in this light. They were simply dark and shaggy. He looked down into a white-walled courtyard with tall iron gates. He was high up—this was an attic room.

Military vehicles stood in the courtyard, jeeps, a canvas-topped truck to transport troops, a rocket launcher—all of them hard-used, except for the Blazer with the pintle mount on its roof. They stood at careless angles around a white plaster decorative fountain that had no water in it. Men in olive drab fatigues and caps leaned against the vehicles or sat on fenders, smoking, talking softly. Only the sibilance of their words reached him, not the vowels, not the sense. Some of them cradled rifles in their arms, some Uzi-style machine guns. They weren't going to let him climb down from this window on knotted sheets, were they?

He turned back. A gaunt man in camouflage pants, a blousy camouflage jacket over a khaki undershirt, looked at him from the doorway of the room. He was old, but he stood straight. Feverishly bright eyes looked at Dave from dark sockets. The man made a try at a smile, and the effect was macabre. "Good morning," he said. "You can shower and shave down the hall." He jerked his head on a stringy neck. "Then I'd like you to join us for breakfast, downstairs. The man on the steps will escort you."

"I'd like him to escort me home," Dave said.

Zorn offered a hand. "Let me introduce myself."

"Colonel Lothrop Zorn." Dave ignored the hand. "U.S. Marine Corps, retired. Only not quite."

Zorn drew back his hand. "Not while my country needs me."

"You embarrassed your country by mining that harbor in Los Inocentes," Dave said. "Your country doesn't need you. Your country doesn't want you. That's why you're here."

"Congress is full of communists," Zorn said. "Calling themselves Democrats and Republicans doesn't change that. I don't care what traitors want. The enemy is at our gates. They know that as well as I do. The difference is, they want to fling the gates open. I want to defend the gates. To the last drop of American blood."

"Or Inocentian blood," Dave said.

"We're all Americans in this hemisphere. President Monroe understood that." Zorn turned away. "Breakfast's at seven. Don't be late." He moved out of sight down the hall. Dave leaned out the doorway. Zorn's scruffy head disappeared down a staircase, watched by a young brown-skinned soldier with a semi-automatic .45 in a holster on his hip. Dave looked up the hall. Another brown-skinned soldier with a gun smiled at him from beside an open bathroom door. "Towels, razor, everything you need is inside, *señor,*" he said.

He wanted to be late, so he took his time showering and shaving. The fixtures in this bathroom were old, a claw-footed bathtub, nicks in its graying enamel, fitted up with a shower of raw pipe, the shower head a recent buy. The washbasin was gray and chipped as the tub but the faucets were new, if cheap. The toilet had a high water tank, the flush activated by a much-painted handle on the end of a chain. Oiled paper made the panes of the window opaque. Maybe the maids who'd lived up here when the house was somebody's had worried about hikers on the slopes using binoculars to watch them.

Clean clothes had been left for him. They lay on a hamper, a big, raveling basket. The clothes were much-washed army fatigues—army underwear first, olive drab. He didn't want to wear these, but he'd sweated his own clothes. He didn't want to put on yesterday's underwear. As to his suit—who knew what kind of day Zorn had planned for him? He checked his watch. Five past seven. He flapped into the clean clothes, slowly, put his wallet and other possessions into the pockets, lit a cigarette, and stepped into the hall. The soldier there looked worried, read his own watch, a ten-dollar digital, and said in Spanish:

"He hates for his guests to be late for meals."

"I'll take the blame," Dave said.

The soldier only gave a sharp tilt to his head, meaning Dave was to go ahead of him to the stairs. The soldier's hand rested on the butt of his pistol. Dave went ahead of him to the stairs and down the stairs. They were of bare wood and narrow. Here and there, thin brass rods showed they had once been carpeted—not for comfort but to dampen the noise of the maids' shoes running up and down. What lunatic had built this monster Spanish Mediterranean up here back of nowhere? Why? This kind of house belonged in La Jolla, Beverly Hills, San Marino. Just to haul the red tiles for the roofs up here must have cost a mint.

The soldier nodded him down a hallway past half a dozen bedrooms. The doors stood open. Locker room smells came out. He glimpsed rows of cots like the one he'd slept on, all neatly made up, a footlocker under each one. Upright lockers of brown metal lined the walls. He saw no nude photographs clipped from magazines and taped to the walls—an American flag now and then, the flag of Los Inocentes, with its Lamb of God. A photo of El Presidente chatting with the U.S. President. The U.S. President grinning and waving from a helicopter on the White House lawn. They reached the front staircase, its steps of flower-painted tile, railings of black wrought iron. Faded rectangles in the stairwell showed where big paintings must have hung long ago.

From the entryway at the foot of the stairs, what had once been a handsome and very large living room was half armory, half gym—racks of guns, exercise equipment, gray floor mats, a howitzer sitting in the fireplace. The smell of neat's foot oil hung in the air, mixed with the smells of the old house, mold, mildew, dust, dry rot, neglect. Floorboards creaked under his shoes as he moved past the stairway, past a long refectory where, under high hand-hewn rafters, soldiers messed at a long plank table, laughed, smoked, argued. In Spanish. Utensils rattled metal plates. A drinking glass broke.

The soldier nodded Dave through a vast, steamy kitchen where young men in skivvy shirts and wrap-around aprons washed dishes at deep metal sinks, and where other young men with their heads wrapped in white thumped bread dough on butcher-block counters, arms coated in flour. Behind the kitchen was a breakfast room with windows all around. Clear morning mountain sunlight slanted through these windows and touched two men who ate at a round table with a white cloth and china plates and cups and saucers. One of the men was Lothrop Zorn, who held his fork in his right hand. The other, who held his fork in his left hand, was General Cortez-Ortiz.

## 17

DAVE SAID, "GENERAL? Do you miss your dog?"

Zorn snapped, "You're late. Sit down." Zorn looked at the soldier. "Mr. Brandstetter's breakfast is on a plate in a warming oven. If you can find it, bring it to him."

The soldier saluted and went back into the kitchen. Dave sat down. Cortez-Ortiz smiled with those white, ferocious teeth. "Which dog is that, *señor*?"

"A young Doberman bitch I saw you playing with in a television film clip. On a patio. In Tegucigalpa."

"Ah." Cortez-Ortiz nodded. "That was the dog of my generous host, the Guatemalan ambassador. A splendid beast." He stretched a hand across the table. "You see what she did to me the moment the cameras stopped?" A long scar ran white across the back of the hand. "They have teeth like razors, those dogs."

"Did you shoot her," Dave said, "or kick her to death?"

Zorn cut in hastily, "What do you think of my layout here, Brandstetter? Not bad, considering I get no support from Washington, right? All private donations."

"I hope you'll show me around," Dave said.

"The dog, *señor*," Cortez-Ortiz said, "is alive and well."

"It's a sad commentary on American life today," Zorn said, "that the men we elect to lead us are prevented from doing that by the very voters who put them into office." The soldier came back, set a plate in front of Dave, pulled aluminum foil off it, and went away with the foil. "Only private citizens are free to act on their convictions."

"If they're rich enough." The scrambled eggs were moist and tasted real. The bacon was just right. The toast was limp, but he was hungry. He slathered it with marmalade and devoured it and the rest greedily. *The condemned man ate a hearty breakfast.* "But your supporters are losing heart, I hear. They think it's time the President got to doing what they bought him the office to do."

"Clean our backyard of Soviet influence," Zorn said. "What do you mean, "rich enough"? You're rich. Plenty."

Dave stared. "Surely you didn't bring me here to coax a donation out of me." It hadn't crossed his mind, but maybe Zorn was crazy enough for it to have crossed his. "I'm afraid it's not the charity of my choice, Colonel."

"I don't want your money," Zorn said.

Dave swallowed coffee. "In that case, there's no need for me to stay." He ate with attention, expecting no answer and getting none. He finished his food, wiped his mouth, laid the napkin beside his plate, lit a cigarette, tucked pack and lighter away, and told Zorn, "I want to go home."

"I am with you in this," Cortez-Ortiz said. He drew smoke from a long slim brown cigar and sighed. "Exile is painful. I miss my wife, my daughters. Lovely girls, *señor*. Flowers. A pity you cannot meet them."

"You think I like being stalled here?" Zorn said. "I have work to do in the world. Work nobody else has the balls for. We've got to wait, that's all. No choice."

"What if they never show up?" Dave said.

Zorn eyed him coldly. "Who are you talking about?"

"The rebels from Los Inocentes, who you made sure know you've got the general here, and who want to try him for the deaths he ordered—of three or four hundred farmers, villagers, Indians, grandmothers, politicians, and little children."

"Lies, *señor*," Cortez-Ortiz said. "Propaganda. These communists—lying is part of their system, their atheistic philosophy. The end justifies the means. How an archbishop could sanction such godlessness is incredible."

"He had to be killed, right?" Dave said.

"Our people are deeply religious," Cortez-Ortiz said. "They could not allow such blasphemy to go unpunished."

"Wanting to feed the poor?" Dave said.

Cortez-Ortiz laughed. "You are a sentimentalist, *señor*. Our Lord said, 'The poor you have always with you'—remember?"

Zorn still glared at Dave. Dave said, "What's wrong? You knew I knew. That's why you brought me here. So I couldn't spoil your game—what's it called, "Bang, you're dead"?"

Zorn snorted, "Name me another game worth a man's time."

"It wasn't worth Rafael's time," Dave said.

"He didn't play by the rules," Zorn said. "He deserted."

"You didn't have him executed for desertion," Dave said. "He was going to give away your plans. You should have caught him sooner and brought him back here. Then you wouldn't have had to kill him—and Adam Streeter, too."

"Rafael was killed in a family fight," Zorn said. "Streeter was killed by his legman, Underhill. For a hundred thousand dollars cash. What's the matter with you, Brandstetter? Where's your perspective? Isn't a hundred thousand enough motive for you? It's enough for the police."

"Half a million sounds better to me," Dave said.

Zorn's creased, hollowed-out face didn't have much color. Now even that left it. "What does that mean?"

Dave opened his mouth to answer, and gunfire stuttered outside in the woods. The sound was flat, like shingles slapping together. Zorn scraped his chair back, went to a window, picked up binoculars from the sill, and set them to his eyes. Dave said, "Was I wrong? Are they here?"

"They won't come by day." Zorn didn't lower the binoculars. His breath fogged the glass. "I've got a trainee out there.

Survival exercise. Each man gets a week. On his own. To find out what he's made of. Gun, the clothes on his back—that's about it."

"And hunted all the time?" Dave said.

"All the time," Zorn said. "You don't sleep. You forage but you don't cook—you can't show smoke. And it gets cold at night—you still can't light a fire. You keep moving."

"They're big mountains," Dave said. "Lots of room to run. Hikers die up here when search parties can't find them."

"It's not like that." The gunfire spattered again. Zorn wiped vapor from the glass with his sleeve. A steel jacket button clicked, clicked. He raised the binoculars once more. "They've got to stay within sight of the flagpole here. We can run a signal flag up any time, which means they're to get back down here on the double."

"What if they're hurt out there alone?"

"They've had first aid training—tear up a shirt, use a stick to make a tourniquet. Or a belt. There's no 'what if' about it. I booby-trap the area—bushes with edible berries, springs, the best-worn pathways. Not mines, of course. A little surprise is what they get—maybe a piece of flack, a powder burn. Nobody comes back unhurt."

"Making the game worth playing?" Dave said.

Zorn grunted, set the glasses back on the sill. "What did you mean about half a million dollars?" He came again to the table in his clumsy boots. Not to sit. To stand gripping the back of his chair and glaring at Dave. "No, don't answer that. I know what you meant. How did you find out about it?"

Cortez-Ortiz cleared his throat. "Gentlemen, if you will excuse me?" He rubbed out his cigar in his saucer and got to his feet. He was lithe. They had treated him well, his kidnappers. He wore a white dress uniform with braid and a chest full of ribbons. He looked handsomer than in the television films. He gave Zorn a nod, Dave a nod, each a small smile. "We will meet again, later." He went away from them through the kitchen.

Dave told Zorn, "When your men came to leave the airline ticket in Underhill's house in Venice, they passed up the hundred thousand. It was required, of course, to make the frame-up work. Still, it struck me as self-denial on a large scale. I've been an insurance investigator all my life. You see a lot of human frailty that way. And almost always connected to money. It figured if someone would use a sum like that as mere window-dressing, they were expecting to collect a great deal more in the end."

Zorn went into the kitchen and came back with a glass coffee urn. Without saying anything, he filled Dave's cup and his own, set the pot down, set himself down. He picked up his coffee cup, blew at it, sipped it with withered lips. "I never had any men at Underhill's house in Venice," he said. "But go on."

"I have a witness." Dave tried his own coffee, lit a fresh cigarette, and thought of Cecil, and hoped what the kid meant when he said "out of town" was Nome, Alaska. Dave said to Zorn, "I have another witness who saw your men climb over the roofs of Streeter's condominium, drop into his office on the third floor, and kill him."

"Never happened," Zorn said.

"They cleared every paper out of Streeter's files," Dave said, "so no one could read about what you're up to."

"You're digging your grave," Zorn said.

"I'll leave that to you, thanks," Dave said.

"I used to smoke three, four packs a day," Zorn said. "Now I've got lung cancer. It's killing me. That's why I wish those commie sons of bitches would get here. I haven't got time to fart around. This country is—"

"In grave danger," Dave said. "You told me."

Zorn grunted and held out a skeletal hand. "Let me have one of your cigarettes."

Dave said, "The Surgeon General has determined—"

"That's another thing wrong with this country," Zorn said. He took a cigarette from the pack Dave held out to him, set it in his mouth, sucked a light from Dave's lighter.

And coughed. Hard. Bending forward, pressing a fist to his chest. Dave had never heard a cough to equal it. But the man recovered, sat straight, wiped away tears. "Turned into an old woman, the government has," he said. "Minding everybody's business, trying to protect everybody from everything. Seat belts. Fifty-five-mile-an-hour speed limit." He got up from the table again and left the room. When he came back, he had a bottle of no-name whiskey. He unscrewed the black plastic top and laced his coffee. He raised eyebrows at Dave. Dave didn't know what to do in this situation sober, maybe a drink would help. He nodded and watched the whiskey go into his own cup. "If you drink, don't drive." Zorn sat down again, set the bottle handy. "If you don't drink, how the hell do you work up your nerve to drive? Leash your dog. Hire the handicapped. Goddamned handicapped have got us by the throat. Can't build steps anymore—only wheelchair ramps. And TV? You seen TV? Every week it's a new play about some cripple, or somebody with a crazy disease nobody ever heard of. You know what I did to my TV?"

"Shot it," Dave said.

Zorn actually laughed. "You're damn right." He sobered, leaned forward, blowing smoke out of his nostrils. "Go on about the half million."

"When your men took Streeter's papers," Dave said, and gulped the coffee-whiskey mix, "they forgot to take a reference book—one of those *New York Times* yearbook things he had on his desk. In that, he'd marked a reference to you, and laid in a clipping from a newspaper on how the President was offering a reward of half a million dollars for the capture of terrorists. The two seemed to go together."

"I shot the TV in Carolina," Zorn said. "Two years ago. They promised a John Wayne movie, and instead it's about this quadriplegic who learns to play volleyball with his head. Who cares? Whose problem is that, anyway? I took careful aim, and pow! You haven't heard anything explode until you hear a picture tube explode."

"I'll try it," Dave said, "sometime when I'm bored."

"You do that." Zorn nodded, blew more smoke out his nose, drank deeply of the whiskey-laced coffee. "Sons of bitches kicked me out of Carolina. Said I let a recruit die. Shit. Did he ask my permission to break his neck? And next thing, Congress passes a bill where you can't train foreigners. Aimed right at me. Oh, yes, they've got me in their sights, the commies have. They know who's on to them."

"When the rebels come"—Dave finished his coffee, picked up the whiskey, sloshed the cup half full—"how are you going to capture them? They have to be delivered alive."

"They'll try a raid," Zorn said. "I'll let them come in, then close the old trap on them."

"Won't they be armed?"

"It's a long border, a long seacoast, you can get anything into this country. Including illegals. Ten to twenty of them are here already. Armed? Hell, yes." He nodded to himself once more, and tilted whiskey into his cup. "No one can get up here unseen. And when they make their move, everybody on my team knows what to do. A token defense, a retreat up into the woods. Most of us will already be up there. Then, when they think they've taken this place, down we all come." Zorn reached out for another cigarette. Dave let him have it without saying anything. He furnished the light for it, and Zorn went to coughing again, convulsing, clawing at his chest. Finally it was over. Zorn wiped the tears from his sunken cheeks, the drool from his mouth, drank whiskey, and said in a raw whisper of a voice, "Villanueva is on a ranch in Pauma Valley. He's the leader, you know. Rodrigo Villanueva. I could take him there—a quiet, night operation. But I want the whole bunch, with their rifles, machine guns, grenades. The works. The papers said five hundred thousand, but this will be worth more. They'll pay a million for an action like this."

"Nobody's going to get hurt?" Dave said.

"Not if I can help it. I'm going to wrap them in cotton wool and send them air first class to Washington. What a show it's going to make. Nobody in the country will be talking about anything else. It'll open their eyes to what we're up against—show 'em it's real. Finally, they'll take me seriously. I was right to mine that harbor. They'll see that now. The commie sympathizers will look like the traitors they really are. Castro and the Soviets will skulk out of Central America with their tails between their legs."

"How did you get the general?" Dave said.

"I have friends in the Honduran military," Zorn said.

"Like your friends in the county sheriff 's office?"

Zorn ignored that. "They believe in me. They lent me a helicopter, whatever I needed. Unofficially, of course."

"Of course." Dave drank from his cup. "What tipped you that Streeter was on to you? Not Rafael. You were surveiling Streeter before that. You knew all about his movements."

"Down in Inocentes, the *chuchos* intercepted a young reporter Streeter had sent to ask the rebels where the general was. Streeter figured they knew. I don't know why."

"Rue Glendenning," Dave said. "His father blamed Streeter for the boy's death and tried to kill him. But you know about that. He wrote a threatening letter. It's among Streeter's papers. He'd like it back. Give it to me and I'll return it to him."

"I don't know anything about any papers." Zorn poured whiskey into his cup. "Anyway, after that I kept an eye on Streeter. He hated my guts, you know. The feeling was mutual. Son of a bitch." Zorn wagged his head grimly and drank. "Goddam writers. Sit safe in an office typing all day, tearing down the men who change things, the real men."

"He traveled to the hot spots all the time," Dave said.

"And never understood them," Zorn said. "Take Los Inocentes for example. Killing is a way of life down there. An ancient tradition." He twisted out his cigarette in the grease on his plate. "Happened before in this century, you know—nineteen thirty-two. People forget. Wholesale murder. Thousands killed—men, women, children. It's in the Indian blood, Brandstetter. The old Feathered Serpent priests, before the Spaniards landed, used to sacrifice hundreds of victims every day, cut their living hearts out with jade knives."

"A pity you had to miss it," Dave said.

Zorn snorted. "It was a way of controlling population growth. Too many mouths to feed. Poor soil. No rain. It's the same today. Read the figures. Seven kids per couple. Nothing to eat. They don't know it, but that's why they keep killing each other."

"And what's your excuse?" Dave said.

"The Soviets and the Cubans lie to them, promise to feed them. If you're hungry, you'll believe anybody. They'll let them in—Nicaragua already has. And soon this country will be finished. It's got to be stopped, and I'm out to stop it."

"With a measly million dollars? You're kidding."

"I'm not like that gang in Washington, all talk, no action." He drank off the whiskey in his cup, rattled the cup into the saucer, tottered to his feet. "Come on. I'll show you around. You'll see how far a little money can be made to go by somebody who really cares."

"Are you going to show me Porfirio too?" Dave asked.

Zorn moved off. "You wouldn't enjoy it," he said.

## 18

DAVE WOKE AND wondered why. And remembered how Zorn had drunk at that table in the breakfast room after dinner while they played stupid hand after hand of some crazy brand of poker whose rules seemed to keep changing with every hand dealt. Zorn was dying of cancer and trying to kill the pain with the whiskey. Dave wasn't dying of anything. Why had he matched the colonel drink for drink? It always woke him this way—too much booze. This room had a ceiling light socket but no bulb. He reached from the bed to grope his watch and lighter from the chair where they lay on his clothes. By the flame of the lighter he read the watch. Three ten. The night was dark. Also cold. He put the lighter and watch back and dragged the camouflage jacket off the chair to put it on, and an engine thrashed to life in the courtyard below. Very loud and sudden it sounded.

He kicked into the camouflage trousers and went to open the window and look down. Men scurried around the courtyard, men with guns on straps. A second engine started, a third. No lights. The only lights were the tiny red coals of cigarettes. But he heard a metallic squeak and thought it came from the hinges of the tall gates to the courtyard. The blurred black shadow of the troop carrier truck moved with a grinding of gears. There was an arch of white stucco over the gate. It shone ghostly in the dark and helped him make out the truck sliding beneath it. A jeep followed it, overloaded with men, dark gun barrels glinting. Another full jeep rolled out, trailing the rocket launcher. A third followed, fenders scraping tires, dragging the howitzer. Boots scraped steps. Zorn spoke and coughed. Car doors slammed, and the Blazer moved out after the other vehicles. It was easier to see because it was shiny.

Dave sat on the bed to pull on socks and boots. On the floor below, men began running in boots. The framework of the house was eaten away by rot and termites, and the movement of so many men together made it shake. He pushed wallet, keys, change, cigarettes, lighter into pockets, strapped on the watch, put on his khaki cap. He laid his own clothes on the bed, and carried the chair to the door. He rapped the door with his knuckles and called, "Guard? I have to go to the bathroom." No reply. He pounded the door. "Guard? I have to go to the bathroom. At once." He heard the boots of the men out in the courtyard now. Only the boots. Running. No other sound. Not a word. It was eerie. "Guard? I am sick. I am going to vomit. I must get to the bathroom."

Boots came up the wooden staircase, jarred the floor of the narrow hallway. A key scraped the lock. The door opened inward but no light came in. Zorn had either closed down the gasoline-powered generator that gave feeble electricity to the place or simply issued a blackout order. But Dave made out the blousy shape of the soldier who stepped hesitantly into the room, and he brought the chair down as hard as he could on the boy's head. The boy moaned and slumped to the floor. Dave flung the chair away, knelt, and yanked the automatic from the boy's holster. His heart pounded; it was difficult to breathe. He put his head into the hallway. No one. He pulled the door shut after him, locked the door, and pocketed the key.

Back to the wall, he edged along the hallway to the stair head. He squinted down into darkness and strained to hear. The only sounds came faintly from outdoors, the scuffle of boots on soil. Zorn's troops were running up into the pines to hide. Soon even these sounds faded out. Somewhere nearby, Zorn's token force waited for the oncoming rebels, but they were dead quiet. Dave pumped a shell from the clip into the chamber. The metallic noise echoed in the stairwell. Holding the pistol ready, he started down the stairs. The treads creaked, snapped, squealed. Each time, he stopped and waited, but no one came. In the second-floor hallway, he turned for the two large bedrooms at the rear. He moved quietly, but if he was right about Lothrop Zorn's plans, there was no need.

The first room was Zorn's. At the second, he stopped and knocked on the door. "General Cortez-Ortiz?" No answer came, and he tried the knob, pushed the door. It was locked. But the lock on his own door above was as simple as a lock can be, and he wondered if maybe all the bedroom doors were the same. He dug the key from his pocket. In the dark, he used his fingers to locate the keyhole in its corroded metal plate, and stuck the key in. It turned. He opened the door. "General? Are you here?" He didn't want to walk into what the soldier upstairs had walked into. He took out his lighter, thumbed it, held the flame up. Cortez-Ortiz lay on a cot on the far side of the room. In the same kind of army surplus skivvies as Dave had been given to wear. He was gagged with a tight white handkerchief. His hands were tied by web belts to the steel-pipe head of the cot, his ankles to the steel- pipe foot. Dave pushed the gun into the waist of his trousers, went to the cot, unstrapped the general's wrists, unknotted the gag, unstrapped his ankles. Cortez-Ortiz did not look svelte in the flicker of Dave's lighter, and he moaned as he struggled to sit up. He swung his legs to the floor, and sat on the cot's edge, bent forward, elbows on knees, hands clutching his head. "He left me here to be killed," he said.

"I figured he would." Dave clicked the lighter off. The windows of the room let a little starlight in. "If they actually killed you, that would make his capture that much more heroic—worth that much more money. It's money he's after, you know. He's not a patriot. And he's not crazy. He's just another hustler with a surefire racket. You were going to jack the take up for him. Double it. From five hundred thousand to a million."

"Not I." Cortez-Ortiz sat straight, took a deep breath, got to his feet. "Not I, but my bullet-riddled corpse." He reached for his white uniform that lay crumpled on the floor. "Thank you, *señor*, for rescuing me." He kicked into his trousers. "We must escape from this place, and there is no time to waste." He sat on the bed again to put on socks and shoes. "What is your plan of action?"

"You were a field officer once," Dave said.

"You have read about me?" Cortez-Ortiz tied the laces of white shoes, sat straight, looked at Dave. His eyes were dark blurs in the pale blur of his face but he sounded pleased as a child to be so famous. "Why, *señor*?"

"I thought we might meet," Dave said. "Do you know explosives—how to rig them?"

"I am not an expert." Cortez-Ortiz retrieved his shirt from the floor and flapped into it. "But I know the rudiments."

"Good. Get your jacket. Let's go."

The cellar had not been much to begin with. Builders in California knew nothing about cellars. It held a bulky old furnace wrapped in layers of smoky asbestos, big pipes reaching out of it in all directions, crawling overhead laden with grime and cobwebs. It had probably burned coal once, then in the 1930s been fitted with an oil burner that now was crusty with rust. Nothing else was in the cellar but stacked crates—ammunition for pistols, rifles, machine guns. Mortar shells, rockets, hand grenades. Dynamite. Materials whose labels told Dave nothing. The crates were stenciled mostly in English, French, Hebrew, but a few in Russian. Dave grinned. Among the crates of rifles were both M-16s and Kalashnikovs. The blackout had been by order, not by switching off the generator. A forty-watt bulb hung from a frayed cord among the ponderous ceiling ducts, and by its weak, watery light Cortez-Ortiz, kneeling on a filthy floor, used pliers, wire cutters, pincers to rig a bomb from sticks of dynamite, a detonator, a timer. His hands shook as he worked. The back of his shirt darkened with sweat. "It has been many years since I have done this, *señor*. The fingers lose their cunning. But I have not forgotten. I remember—just—what—to do." He grinned up at Dave for a second. "And it is a pleasure." He gave a final twist to a screw, dropped the tools with a rattle, and stood, brushing his hands. "Finished." With his foot, he pushed the thing up against a stack of crates. He took his jacket from where it hung on a corner of a crate, and shrugged into it. "In seven minutes, this house will cease to exist."

"Thank you." Dave moved toward the cellar steps. "A boy is locked in upstairs. I can't leave him there."

"*Señor!*" Cortez-Ortiz reached for him. "The time."

"I'll make it," Dave said. "I have to."

He took the steps two at a time. Looming stoves, bread racks, counters, cupboards, rolling food carts made an obstacle course of the kitchen. Then he was on the wooden back stairs. He couldn't take these two at a time. The spring was out of his legs. His wind was gone. His heart banged in his chest as if it wanted out. He wasn't going to make it to the top. He had to stop and catch his breath. Cortez-Ortiz was younger, probably by ten years. He came on up.

"Are you ill?"

"Just out of shape," Dave gasped.

"I will go," Cortez-Ortiz said, and went.

Dave called after him, "Top floor, end of the hall, by the bathroom." He swallowed in a dry throat, braced a hand on the wall, and began to climb again. But slowly. His legs were leaden. He reached the second floor, and Cortez-Ortiz, little more than a white blur, came down to him, fancy shoes rattling the steps. He caught a heel, almost fell.

"He broke the door," he panted. "He is not there."

"Good," Dave said. "Let's go."

And gunfire, a lot of it, began out beyond the front of the house.

"*Madre de Dios,*" Cortez-Ortiz said. "They have come." He looked this way, that way, panicky. "Where can we go?"

"Don't worry," Dave said, "it will end in a minute."

"We have very few minutes at our disposal, *señor.*"

"Right. Come on." Dave headed for the front staircase. Cortez-Ortiz caught his jacket. "Not that way."

"There's no cover out the back," Dave said. "We'd be clear targets for Zorn up there on the slopes." He moved on past the open doors of the barrack like bedrooms. "There's confusion out front. Maybe we won't be noticed."

Cortez-Ortiz remained planted in the hallway, hands to his head. "Is there no other choice?"

Dave turned back at the top of the stairs. "There's one. Stay here and be blown up. Come on, general."

Cortez-Ortiz moaned, but he moved. Dave started down the stairs, and the general's beautiful shoes clattered on the tiles behind him. A mortar fired outside. Rifles snapped. Machine guns stammered. Flames crackled. And there came another sound. It so surprised Dave that he stopped. Cortez-Ortiz bumped into him. Dave turned his head to look into his face. "Do you hear what I think I hear?"

Cortez-Ortiz squinted. "You mean the helicopter?"

"It doesn't fit," Dave said. "Come on." He turned at the jog in the stairs, took two more steps down, and jerked to a halt. Cortez-Ortiz behind him drew in his breath. One of Zorn's *chuchos* stood in the doorway, holding an Uzi. Outside, something was burning, not in the courtyard itself but just beyond the gate. Dave couldn't see what it was from here. Probably one of Zorn's battered trucks. Whatever it was, it threw a strong, fitful red light. And by that light Dave saw the young man's face, surprised, delighted, saw him aim the gun, saw his mouth spread in a laugh. He squeezed the trigger. Flame spurted from the barrel with each bullet. The bullets ricocheted, whining, off the flowered tiles of the staircase. For how long—half a second? Then they stopped. The young man toppled face forward into the entry hall, the gun clattering and spinning away from him across the tiles.

Two figures in jeans came at a run through the door. Dave knew the tall one right away, the one who shouted "Dave?" It was Cecil. He had the SIG Sauer automatic in his hand.

The other was Bobby Shales. He held an Uzi. In a way that said he could use it again. "Come on, Mr. Brandstetter," he said.

Dave said, "Come on, general," and turned. Cortez-Ortiz lay sprawled on his back on the stairs, five holes across the chest of his white jacket. His eyes were open, staring at nothing. Dave ran down the stairs. He grabbed Shales's arm, Cecil's arm. "Run like hell," he said. "This place is going to blow up."

The big brown helicopter swung wide circles over the ragged, burning ruins of Zorn's house. The flames leaped high. Dave could feel the heat through the curved glass of the chopper. By the light of the fire, Duke Summers, in a flak jacket, studied detail maps on his knees, an officer in uniform leaning over him. Summers wore a headset, barked orders into it, listened, cursed, barked again. Dave judged he was having the time of his life. He and Cecil and Shales stared silently out the window at the action below. It was like a scene in hell. Dante would have loved it. Zorn's guards had been loaded into trucks that were already tilting down the narrow crooked road among the big trees. Spurts of gunfire, the swing of spotlights up the tree-grown slopes showed that Summers's people were rounding up the rest of Zorn's men. With a grimace, Summers pulled off the headset. Dave shouted at him over the clamor of the rotors:

"Didn't I say you could do anything you wanted?"

"I couldn't let Zorn kill you," Summers said.

Dave grinned. "Not when a good-looking young man came begging for your help."

Shales's poker face almost cracked a smile. Summers scowled and glanced nervously at the officer and the pilot. "I don't know what you're talking about."

Dave asked Cecil, "What tipped you to where I was?"

"Not where you were," Cecil said, "but who had you. Hilda Vosper. She saw the Blazer drive off with you in the back. I got home just after that. She was walking back with her dog, and saw me, and told me. It worried her. She said you didn't look like you were sleeping—you looked hurt. I figured she was right. El Coronel's commandos had you, didn't they? And what was I to do? Couldn't locate Leppard. Out of his bailiwick anyhow. Came to me you said you knew Duke Summers, and he lived at the Grovers. Closed up tight—but not the kitchen. I was invisible, wasn't I? Put on a white coat, picked up a bucket of ice, and went to find Mr. Duke Summers."

"You're young for a Grovers waiter," Dave said.

"Bobby thought so, too." Cecil grinned at Shales, who again almost smiled. "But I sweet-talked him, didn't I?"

"We knew how to find this place," Shales said. "Sorry it took so long to muster troops and ordnance."

"Not too long," Dave said, "thank God." He gave Summers a wry salute.

Summers grouched, "This could cost me my career."

"Crying on your cot again?" Dave said. "You saved Washington half a million dollars. They'll give you a medal." He turned to Cecil. "Just as a matter of curiosity, where were you, day before yesterday? Where did you go?"

"Vegas," Cecil said. "Somebody had to save Chrissie. She couldn't go back to her mother's. Brenda was going to rip her off. Ken was going to rape her. County wanted to put her in a foster home."

Dave stared. "You married her."

Cecil grinned. "You got it."

*Continue reading for a preview of the next*
*Dave Brandstetter novel*

He crossed airport tarmac in the rain, and climbed a cold, wet steel staircase to a DC-8. He had been waiting for this. Six days in Fresno were plenty. The death claims division of Sequoia Life had been right in their suspicions. They had hired him to find proof that what looked like death by accident in a fire at a small printing plant had been murder. The wife had killed the husband for his insurance. But digging out the proof had been slow going.

The aircraft smelled stale inside. Freshener sprayed through the ducts was trying to dispel the spent breath and smoke and body warmth of the load of passengers who had just gotten off, but the crowd boarding with him was bringing new smells of rain-damp clothing. He stowed attaché case and raincoat in an overhead compartment, then settled into a window seat and buckled his belt. The seat was in the non-smoking section. He was trying to quit.

The plane sat for half an hour by the terminal, and another twenty minutes out on a runway. Dave looked up from the pages of the in-flight magazine, now and then to gaze off at the rainy outline of the Sierras looming to the east. The plane lifted off, rain hissing against the small windows, at 10:40 A.M., and touched down in the rain at

LAX at 11:25, so there was still something left of the day. Standing, waiting, at the luggage-go-round, he forgot and lit a cigarette, then remembered and dropped it and put a foot on it.

Outside, under a massive gray concrete overhang, he stood on cement, attaché case and grip at his feet, the raincoat hung over his shoulders because it was cold and damp as a tomb here. He watched cab drivers and airport cops scream at each other, watched jitneys stop and take on hotel-bound arrivals, watched passenger cars jockey for spaces at the curbs. Finally he saw Cecil's flame-painted van, glossy with rain, picked up the bags, jogged to where it waited for him, the horns of twenty cars clamoring behind it. Cecil leaned across, opened the door, grabbed the bags, dumped them into the back of the van. Dave climbed in and slammed the door. Cecil gave him a kiss, put the van in gear, they moved on, and the honking stopped—most of it. They inched along for a time in bumper-to-bumper traffic, then were on a broad, curving stretch of roadway swinging past looming glass and metal buildings, office complexes, hotels. Then they were on a boulevard and pointed northward. And Cecil said, "I was glad to get your call. Those taxi drivers, from what I hear, they'll take you for every dime before they let you out at home. Drive you to Northridge, just to run up the meter."

"Tell me about it," Dave said. "Thanks for coming."

Cecil stared ahead past the swinging windshield wipers that pushed aside the rain, pushed aside the rain, pushed aside the rain. Red traffic lights glowed at a broad intersection. He braked the van, glanced at Dave, and said, "I'll come anytime you ask, anywhere. You know that."

Dave nodded curtly. "I know that."

"All you have to do"—Cecil moved the gearshift lever—"is ask." The signal switched to go. He moved the van on across the intersection, and started it up a long slope 'tween green hills where abandoned oil pumps rusted in the rain. "I keep waiting for you to ask." He was a tall, gangly, good-looking black who worked as a field reporter in television news. He was twenty-five years old. Dave had met him on a case up the central coast a few years back. Later they had settled in together in Dave's house. And worked together. Until Cecil had been shot almost to death, until Cecil had been forced to kill a man to save Dave's life. After that he had gone back to the newsroom. Tried. But another case had forced him to help out again. He was smart and resourceful and had got Dave out of trouble.

But he had made trouble for himself. It was still not over.

"You want to come back?" Dave said. "Come back. You were the one who left. It wasn't my idea."

"It was your idea to take Chrissie in," Cecil said.

"It was your idea to marry her." Dave lit a cigarette with shaking hands. "I only wanted to shelter her till things could be worked out by the courts."

"The courts." Cecil stopped himself, pressed his mouth tight, drew in air through his nose. The van topped the long rise, and below lay the west side of the city, stretching miles in the rain, under tattered clouds, mountains off to the north, shrouded in mist. Cecil said, keeping tight control over his voice, "Did anybody ever tell you, you have ice water in your veins?"

"Several people." Dave blew away smoke, groped for and found the ashtray in the blue dash. "On several occasions. Always when they knew I was right and they were wrong. Emotions doesn't change facts. And they hated believing that."

"I've told you from the start, it wasn't emotion," Cecil said. "Her father was dead, murdered, the only one who loved and cared for her. Her grandmother wouldn't have let her come to harm, but she was dead, too. Her damned mother wanted to control her so she could control all that money Chrissie had coming. You know what her mother is. Her mother's boyfriend tried to rape Chrissie. The County wanted to put her in a foster home. Somebody had to do something."

"You've told me," Dave said.

"It was a cool, calculated decision," Cecil said. "No emotion involved. Except yours. It only took a day to drive her to Las Vegas and marry her, so she'd be her own boss, and nobody could rip her off. She's blind, Dave. She's only seventeen years old, for Christ sake."

"And that day," Dave said, "was the first day of the rest of your life—right?"

"No way." Cecil shook his head hard. "Dave, she'll get over it. It's a teenage infatuation. She'll get tired of me and ask out." He braked the van behind a long line of rain-washed cars at the foot of the grade. "Not the rest of my life—no."

"Yes—unless you tell her. You should never have let her take you to bed. You've got brains that absolutely stagger me. How could you be so stupid?"

"She was sad and lost and alone in the dark," Cecil said. "She needed somebody to hold her."

"And you think she's going to get tired of that?"

"You did," Cecil said. "You shut me right out."

"It was your decision, not mine," Dave said. "You are the dearest thing in life to me. You're bright and funny and gentle and decent and full of life. And I will never get tired of you, and neither will Chrissie. It's not up to her anyway. You're the adult. Tell her the truth—that it was an act of kindness that got out of hand."

"I can't hurt her like that," Cecil said.

"It will hurt more the longer you let it go on."

"Dave, she needs somebody who gives a damn."

"And sex is the only way to convey that?" Dave asked.

"It beats gin rummy," Cecil said. The cars ahead began to crawl. He shifted gears and followed. The rain-sleek band of white concrete bent westward. He touched a signal switch and eased the van into the leftmost lane. He would use the Santa Monica Freeway on-ramp at La Cienega. "Dave, what do you want from me?"

Dave laughed bleakly, twisted out his cigarette, pushed the ashtray shut with a clack. "You'll brace anybody—truck bombers, homicidal maniacs, terrorists. But you haven't got the guts to tell one young girl the truth."

"It's not the same thing," Cecil said, "and you know it."

"And you know what I want from you," Dave said. "I want you to stop living a lie."

"I'm not living a stupid lie," Cecil shouted. "I'm not sleeping around. God knows, I'm not sleeping with you."

"God may not," Dave said, "but I sure as hell do."

"Yeah, well, that's how you wanted it. You made the rules. Only you're forgetting one today, aren't you? You weren't going to talk to me like this. It was none of your business. It was up to me to sort it out and do the honest thing, right?"

"Right. But I didn't know it would take you months." The blue velvet passenger seat was on a swivel. Dave turned it so as to face Cecil. "You know what I've begun to think sometimes, these nights alone? That I was wrong. When you came to find me, and said you wanted to stay, I thought this is nice but it can't last. He's young, he'll move on. But then I got to know you, and like a fool I let myself believe we had a bond between us nothing could break."

"We did." Tears ran down Cecil's face. "We do."

"Don't do that." Dave reached across and wiped away the tears with his fingers. "Nature decides. We like to think we can control it, but we can't." He swiveled the seat again, stared woodenly ahead. Past the moving wipers, cars crawled up the freeway on-ramp between banks of rain-washed ground ivy. "So, now it's Chrissie's turn. Lucky Chrissie." He forced a smile. "Well, you and I had four good years. When we get home, we'll drink to that. One last drink together."

"God damn you," Cecil said.

And no one said anything after that for a long while. Cecil jounced the van down into the yard of Dave's place from crooked, climbing Horseshoe Canyon Trail. Shrubs and trees here dripped onto uneven brick paving and made puddles. Dave's brown Jaguar stood by the long row of French doors that were the face of the front building. The storm had strewed the car with leaves and twigs.

It was noon, but the light here was dusky when they got down from the van, and Cecil dragged out of it Dave's grip and attaché case. Dave draped the trenchcoat over his shoulders again, and followed Cecil as he rounded the shingled end of the front building to a bricked courtyard shadowed by the gnarled branches of an old California oak. Cecil made a sound, stopped in his tracks, Dave blundered against him and banged a shin on the suitcase. He opened his mouth to ask, then didn't have to ask. He saw what Cecil saw.

A circular wooden bench hugged the thick trunk of the oak. On the bench stood potted plants. But a space had been left in case anyone wanted to sit on the bench. And a man was seated there. He leaned back against the tree trunk, head lolling to one side, hands open in his lap. The rain had soaked his hair and clothes, tweed jacket, wool slacks, good shoes.

"Is he asleep?" Cecil said.

"In this weather? If he is, he must be drunk." Dave went to the man, bent over him. His eyes were closed, but he wasn't asleep. He wasn't breathing. A pink stain was on his shirt, to the left of the breastbone. The rain had washed the bright red away, but it was a bloodstain. Dave laid fingers against the man's face. "He's dead."

"What's this?" Cecil bent and picked up something white and soggy and small from the wet bricks at the man's feet. A business card. He squinted at it in the gray light, gave a soft grunt, and passed the card to Dave. Dave dug reading glasses from a jacket pocket, put the glasses on, and read the printing on the card. He blinked surprise. "It's mine," he said, and put the reading glasses away.

"Who is he?" Cecil said.

"Beats me," Dave said. "Come on. He's sat here too long already." He moved toward a rear building, almost the same as the front ones, long and low. Both had been stables in some far gone past. The front one was now a rangy living room, the rear one had lofts for sleeping, a long couch in front of a big fireplace, Dave's desk and files. "He's cold as ice. Must have been here all night." He fitted a key into a door, pushed the door, and moved down the long room between knotty pine walls under naked pine rafters, to lift the receiver from the telephone on his desk. "At least all night. Maybe longer than that. Maybe days."

"Wouldn't the coyotes have found him?" Cecil laid the attaché case on the desk, and carried the grip up raw pine stairs to the north loft. "What do you think? Could they smell him in the rain?"

"They didn't." Dave sniffed his fingers. They smelled of the man's cologne. And tobacco. He lit a cigarette and waited, phone to his ear, to get through to Jefferson Leppard, Lieutenant, Homicide Division, LAPD. Leppard was a blunt-shaped, blunt-spoken young black with a passion for high-style clothes.

"Brandstetter?" he said. "I hope it's simple."

"I doubt it," Dave said. "I have a body for you."

"What kind of body?" Leppard said.

"The dead kind," Dave said. "Sitting in my patio."

"I meant, give me a description," Leppard said.

"Male, well-dressed, about thirty-five years old, fair hair, weight about one thirty, height about five eleven, a stab wound in the chest."

"You didn't touch it." Leppard sounded alarmed.

"I only touched his skin to check his temperature," Dave said. "He didn't have a temperature."

"Right," Leppard said. "This sounds like number six."

"I guess you'll have to explain that to me," Dave said.

Cecil came down the stairs at a loose-jointed run, sideways, two steps at a time. He lifted the coat from Dave's shoulders, took it to a standing rack by the bar under the north sleeping loft. He hung the coat up, and began to rattle bottles. Dave sat in the desk chair and told Leppard:

"I've been out of town. Up in Fresno for a week. On a case. Arson to cover murder. I just now got back. Cecil picked me up at the airport. What do you mean—number six?"

"We have a new crazy in town," Leppard said. "Serial killer. All stabbings, quick and clean and deadly."

"That's how this one looks—very little blood."

"Victims all young males, in West LA and Hollywood mostly. Any reason for this one to end up at your place?"

"He had my business card," Dave said, "but I don't know him. He must have got the card from someone else."

"Are you gay?" Leppard said.

"I thought you'd never ask," Dave said.

Leppard laughed. "Sorry about that. But it's the connection. All the victims have been gay. We've checked them all out. Families, friends, fellow workers, lovers, bars, bathhouses, hospitals."

"Hospitals?" Dave said.

"That's the other connection," Leppard said. "That's why I was worried you might have touched the wound. It's blood that transmits the virus."

"Are you talking about AIDS?" Dave said.

"They all had it," Leppard said. "Every damned one."

"You coming to collect him?" Dave said.

"With my latex gloves," Leppard said, and hung up.

Cecil set a snifter on the desk. The brandy in it had a golden glow. Dave lifted the fragile bulb of glass and studied it. "Isn't this for after lunch?"

"I'm not staying for lunch. It's brandy because you said it's our last drink, and brandy was what we drank first, the night I blew in here four years ago. Never had brandy before. Remember that night? You got home late. I'd waited hours for you. Sat out there where that dead man is sitting now. In the night like him. Cold like him."

"Not cold like him," Dave said. "Cheers."

"Yeah," Cecil said glumly, "cheers."

And they drank together.

**Joseph Hansen** (1923–2004) was the author of more than twenty-five novels, including the twelve groundbreaking Dave Brandstetter mystery novels. The winner of the 1992 Lifetime Achievement Award from the Private Eye Writers of America, Hansen was also the author of *A Smile in his Lifetime, Living Upstairs, Job's Year,* and *Bohannon's Country.* He was a two-time Lambda Literary Award-winner.